The Book of

by Basil Mathews

CONTENTS

THE BOOK OF MISSIONARY HEROES

PROLOGUE

THE RELAY-RACE

The shining blue waters of two wonderful gulfs were busy with fishing boats and little ships. The vessels came under their square sails and were driven by galley-slaves with great oars.

A Greek boy standing, two thousand years ago, on the wonderful mountain of the Acro-Corinth that leaps suddenly from the plain above Corinth to a pinnacle over a thousand feet high, could see the boats come sailing from the east, where they hailed from the Pires and Ephesus and the marble islands of the Aegean Sea. Turning round he could watch them also coming from the West up the Gulf of Corinth from the harbours of the Gulf and even from the Adriatic Sea and Brundusium.

In between the two gulfs lay the Isthmus of Corinth to which the men on the ships were sailing and rowing.

The people were all in holiday dress for the great athletic sports were to be held on that day and the next,--the sports that drew, in those ancient days, over thirty thousand Greeks from all the country round; from the towns on the shores of the two gulfs and from the mountain-lands of Greece,--from Parnassus and Helicon and Delphi, from Athens and the villages on the slopes of Hymettus and even from Sparta.

These sports, which were some of the finest ever held in the whole world, were called--because they were held on this isthmus--the Isthmian Games.

The athletes wrestled. They boxed with iron-studded leather straps over their knuckles. They fought lions brought across the Mediterranean (the Great Sea as they called it) from Africa, and tigers carried up the Khyber Pass across Persia from India. They flung spears, threw quoits and ran foot-races. Amid the wild cheering of thirty thousand throats the charioteers drove their frenzied horses, lathered with foam, around the roaring stadium.

One of the most beautiful of these races has a strange hold on the imagination. It was a relay-race. This is how it was run.

Men bearing torches stood in a line at the starting point. Each man belonged to a separate team. Away in the distance stood another row of men waiting. Each of these was the comrade of one of those men at the starting point. Farther on still, out of sight, stood another row and then another and another.

At the word "Go" the men at the starting point leapt forward, their torches burning. They ran at top speed towards the waiting men and then gasping for breath, each passed his torch to his comrade in the next row. He, in turn, seizing the flaming torch, leapt forward and dashed along the course toward the next relay, who again raced on and on till at last one man dashed past the winning post with his torch burning ahead of all the others, amid the applauding cheers of the multitude.

The Greeks, who were very fond of this race, coined a proverbial phrase from it. Translated it runs:

"Let the torch-bearers hand on the flame to the others" or "Let those who have the light pass it on."

* * * * *

That relay-race of torch-bearers is a living picture of the wonderful relay-race of heroes who, right through the centuries, have, with dauntless courage and a scorn of danger and difficulty, passed through thrilling adventures in order to carry the Light across the continents and oceans of the world.

The torch-bearers! The long race of those who have borne, and still carry the torches, passing them on from hand to hand, runs before us. A little ship puts out from Seleucia, bearing a man who had caught the fire in a blinding blaze of light on the road to Damascus. Paul crosses the sea and then threads his way through the cities of Cyprus and Asia Minor, passes over the blue Aegean to answer the call from Macedonia. We see the light quicken, flicker and glow to a steady blaze in centre after centre of life, till at last the torch-bearer reaches his goal in Rome.

"Yes, without cheer of sister or of daughter, Yes, without stay of father or of son, Lone on the land and homeless on the water Pass I in patience till the work be done."

Centuries pass and men of another age, taking the light that Paul had brought, carry the torch over Apennine and Alp, through dense forests where wild beasts and wilder savages roam, till they cross the North Sea and the light reaches the fair-haired Angles of Britain, on whose name Augustine had exercised his punning humour, when he said, "Not Angles, but Angels." From North and South, through Columba and Aidan, Wilfred of Sussex and Bertha of Kent, the light came to Britain.

"Is not our life," said the aged seer to the Mercian heathen king as the Missionary waited for permission to lead them to Christ, "like a sparrow that flies from the darkness through the open window into this hall and flutters about in the torchlight for a few moments to fly out again into the darkness of the night. Even so we know not whence our life comes nor whither it goes. This man can tell us. Shall we not receive his teaching?" So the English, through these torch-bearers, come into the light.

The centuries pass by and in 1620 the little Mayflower, bearing Christian descendants of those heathen Angles--new torch-bearers, struggles through frightful tempests to plant on the American Continent the New England that was indeed to become the forerunner of a New World.[1]

A century and a half passes and down the estuary of the Thames creeps another sailing ship.

The Government officer shouts his challenge:

"What ship is that and what is her cargo?"

"The Duff," rings back the answer, "under Captain Wilson, bearing Missionaries to the South Sea."

The puzzled official has never heard of such beings! But the little ship passes on and after adventures and tempests in many seas at last reaches the far Pacific. There the torch-bearers pass from island to island and the light flames like a beacon fire across many a blue lagoon and coral reef.

One after another the great heroes sail out across strange seas and penetrate hidden continents each with a torch in his hand.

Livingstone, the lion-hearted pathfinder in Africa, goes out as the fearless explorer, the dauntless and resourceful missionary, faced by poisoned arrows and the guns of Arabs and marched with only his black companions for thousands of miles through marsh and forest, over mountain pass and across river swamps, in loneliness and hunger, often with bleeding feet, on and on to the little hut in old Chitambo's village in Ilala, where he crossed the river. Livingstone is the Coeur-de-Lion of our Great Crusade.

John Williams, who, in his own words, could "never be content with the limits of a single reef," built with his own hands and almost without any tools on a cannibal island the wonderful little ship The Messenger of Peace in which he sailed many thousands of miles from island to island across the Pacific Ocean.

These are only two examples of the men whose adventures are more thrilling than those of our story books and yet are absolutely true, and we find them in every country and in each of the centuries.

So--as we look across the ages we

"See the race of hero-spirits Pass the torch from hand to hand."

In this book the stories of a few of them are told as yarns to boys and girls round a camp-fire. Every one of the tales is historically true, and is accurate in detail.

In that ancient Greek relay-race the prize to each winner was simply a wreath of leaves cut by a priest with a golden knife from trees in the sacred grove near the Sea,--the grove where the Temple of Neptune, the god of the Ocean, stood. It was just a crown of wild olive that would wither away. Yet no man would have changed it for its weight in gold.

For when the proud winner in the race went back to his little city, set among the hills, with his already withering wreath, all the people would come and hail him a victor and wave ribbons in the air. A great sculptor would carve a statue of him in imperishable marble and it would be set up in the city. And on the head of the statue of the young athlete was carved a wreath.

In the great relay-race of the world many athletes--men and women--have won great fame by the speed and skill and daring with which they carried forward the torch and, themselves dropping in their tracks, have passed the flame on to the next runner; Paul, Francis, Penn, Livingstone, Mackay, Florence Nightingale, and a host of others. And many who have run just as bravely and swiftly have won no fame at all though their work was just as great. But the fame or the forgetting really does not matter. The fact is that the race is still running; it has not yet been won. Whose team will win? That is what matters.

The world is the stadium. Teams of evil run rapidly and teams of good too.

The great heroes and heroines whose story is told in this book have run across the centuries over the world to us. Some of them are alive to-day, as heroic as those who have gone. But all of them say the same thing to us of the new world who are coming after them:

"Take the torch."

The greatest of them all, when he came to the very end of his days, as he fell and passed on the Torch to others, said:

"I have run my course."

But to us who are coming on as Torch-bearers after him he spoke in urgent words--written to the people at Corinth where the Isthmian races were run:

"Do you not know that they which run in a race all run, but one wins the prize? So run, that ye may be victors."

FOOTNOTES:

[Footnote 1: See "The Argonauts of Faith" by Basil Mathews. (Doran.)]

Book One: THE PIONEERS

CHAPTER I

THE HERO OF THE LONG TRAIL

St. Paul

(Dates, b. A.D. 6, d. A.D. 67[2])

The Three Comrades.

The purple shadows of three men moved ahead of them on the tawny stones of the Roman road on the high plateau of Asia Minor one bright, fresh morning.[3] They had just come out under the arched gateway through the thick walls of the Roman city of Antioch-in-Pisidia. The great aqueduct of stone that brought the water to the city from the mountains on their right[4] looked like a string of giant camels turned to stone.

Of the three men, one was little more than a boy. He had the oval face of his Greek father and the glossy dark hair of his Jewish mother. The older men, whose long tunics were caught up under their girdles to give their legs free play in walking, were brown, grizzled, sturdy travellers. They had walked a hundred leagues together from the hot plains of Syria, through the snow-swept passes of the Taurus mountains, and over the sun-scorched levels of the high plateau.[5] Their muscles were as tireless as whipcord. Their courage had not quailed before robber or blizzard, the night yells of the hyena or the stones of angry mobs.

For the youth this was his first adventure out into the glorious, unknown world. He was on the open road with the glow of the sun on his cheek and the sting of the breeze in his face; a strong staff in his hand; with his wallet stuffed with food--cheese, olives, and some flat slabs of bread; and by his side his own great hero, Paul. Their sandals rang on the stone pavement of the road which ran straight as a strung bowline from the city, Antioch-in-Pisidia, away to the west. The boy carried over his shoulder the cloak of Paul, and carried that cloak as though it had been the royal purple garment of the Roman Emperor himself instead of the worn, faded, travel-stained cloak of a wandering tent-maker.

The two older men, whose names were Paul the Tarsian and Silas, had trudged six hundred miles. Their younger companion, whose name was "Fear God," or Timothy as we say, with his Greek fondness for perfect athletic fitness of the body, proudly felt the taut, wiry muscles working under his skin.

On they walked for day after day, from dawn when the sun rose behind them to the hour when the sun glowed over the hills in their faces. They turned northwest and at last dropped down from the highlands of this plateau of Asia Minor, through a long broad valley, until they looked down across the Plain of Troy to the bluest sea in the world.

Timothy's eyes opened with astonishment as he looked down on such a city as he had never seen--the great Roman seaport of Troy. The marble Stadium, where the chariots raced and the gladiators fought, gleamed in the afternoon light.

The three companions could not stop long to gaze. They swung easily down the hill-sides and across the plain into Troy, where they took lodgings.

They had not been in Troy long when they met a doctor named Luke. We do not know whether one of them was ill and the doctor helped him; we do not know whether Doctor Luke (who was a Greek) worshipped, when he met them, 苊 culapius, the god of healing of the Greek people. The doctor did not live in Troy, but was himself a visitor.

"I live across the sea," Luke told his three friends--Paul, Silas and Timothy-- stretching his hand out towards the north. "I live," he would say proudly, "in the greatest city of all Macedonia--Philippi. It is called after the great ruler Philip of Macedonia."

Then Paul in his turn would be sure to tell Doctor Luke what it was that had brought him across a thousand miles of plain and mountain pass, hill and valley, to Troy. This is how he would tell the story in such words as he used again and again:

"I used to think," he said, "that I ought to do many things to oppose the name of Jesus of Nazareth. I had many of His disciples put into prison and even voted for their being put to death. I became so exceedingly mad against them that I even pursued them to foreign cities.

"Then as I was journeying[6] to Damascus, with the authority of the chief priests themselves, at mid-day I saw on the way a light from the sky, brighter than the blaze of the sun, shining round about me and my companions. And, as we were all fallen on to the road, I heard a voice saying to me:

"'Saul, Saul, why do you persecute me? It is hard for you to kick against the goad.'

"And I said, 'Who are you, Lord?'

"The answer came: 'I am Jesus, whom you persecute.'"

Then Paul went on:

"I was not disobedient to the heavenly vision; but I told those in Damascus and in Jerusalem and in all Judea, aye! and the foreign nations also, that they should repent and turn to God.

"Later on," said Paul, "I fell into a trance, and Jesus came again to me and said, 'Go, I will send you afar to the Nations.' That (Paul would say to Luke) is why I walk among perils in the city; in perils in the wilderness; in perils in the sea; in labour and work; in hunger and thirst and cold, to tell people everywhere of the love of God shown in Jesus Christ."[7]

The Call to Cross the Sea.

One night, after one of these talks, as Paul was asleep in Troy, he seemed to see a figure standing by him. Surely it was the dream-figure of Luke, the doctor from Macedonia, holding out his hands and pleading with Paul, saying, "Come over into Macedonia and help us."

Now neither Paul nor Silas nor Timothy had ever been across the sea into the land that we now call Europe. But in the morning, when Paul told his companions about the dream that he had had, they all agreed that God had called them to go and deliver the good news of the Kingdom to the people in Luke's city of Philippi and in the other cities of Macedonia.

So they went down into the busy harbour of Troy, where the singing sailor-men were bumping bales of goods from the backs of camels into the holds of the ships, and they took a passage in a little coasting ship. She hove anchor and was rowed out through the entrance between the ends of the granite piers of the harbour. The seamen hoisting the sails, the little ship went gaily out into the Aegean Sea.

All day they ran before the breeze and at night anchored under the lee of an island. At dawn they sailed northward again with a good wind, till they saw land. Behind the coast on high ground the columns of a temple glowed in the sunlight. They ran into a spacious bay and anchored in the harbour of a new city--Neapolis as it was called--the port of Philippi.

Landing from the little ship, Paul, Silas, Timothy and Luke climbed from the harbour by a glen to the crest of the hill, and then on, for three or four hours of hard walking, till their sandals rang on the pavement under the marble arch of the gate through the wall of Philippi.

Flogging and Prison.

As Paul and his friends walked about in the city they talked with people; for instance, with a woman called Lydia, who also had come across the sea from Asia Minor where she was born. She and her children and slaves all became Christians. So the men and women of Philippi soon began to talk about these strange teachers from the East. One day Paul and Silas met a slave girl dressed in a flowing, coloured tunic. She was a fortune-teller, who earned money for her masters by looking at people and trying to see at a glance what they were like so that she might tell their fortunes. The fortune-telling girl saw Paul and Silas going along, and she stopped and called out loud so that everyone who went by might hear: "These men are the slaves of the Most High God. They tell you the way of Salvation."

The people stood and gaped with astonishment, and still the girl called out the same thing, until a crowd began to come round. Then Paul turned round and with sternness in his voice spoke to the evil spirit in the girl and said: "In the Name of Jesus Christ, I order you out of her."

From that day the girl lost her power to tell people's fortunes, so that the money that used to come to her masters stopped flowing. They were very angry and stirred up everybody to attack Paul and Silas. A mob collected and searched through the streets until they found them. Then they clutched hold of their arms and robes, shouting: "To the priors! To the priors!" The priors were great officials who sat in marble chairs in the Forum, the central square of the city.

The masters of the slave girl dragged Paul and Silas along. At their heels came the shouting mob and when they came in front of the priors, the men cried out:

"See these fellows! Jews as they are, they are upsetting everything in the city. They tell people to take up customs that are against the Law for us as Romans to accept."

"Yes! Yes!" yelled the crowd. "Flog them! Flog them!"

The priors, without asking Paul or Silas a single question as to whether this was true, or allowing them to make any defence, were fussily eager to show their Roman patriotism. Standing up they gave their orders:

"Strip them, flog them."

The slaves of the priors seized Paul and Silas and took their robes from their backs. They were tied by their hands to the whipping-post. The crowd gathered round to see the foreigners thrashed.

The lictors--that is the soldier-servants of the priors--untied their bundles of rods. Then each lictor brought down his rod with cruel strokes on Paul and Silas. The rods cut into the flesh and the blood flowed down.

Then their robes were thrown over their shoulders, and the two men, with their tortured backs bleeding, were led into the black darkness of the cell of the city prison; shackles were snapped on to their arms, and their feet were clapped into stocks. Their bodies ached; the other prisoners groaned and cursed; the filthy place stank; sleep was impossible.

But Paul and Silas did not groan. They sang the songs of their own people, such as the verses that Paul had learned--as all Jewish children did--when he was a boy at school. For instance--

God is our refuge and strength, A very present help in trouble. Therefore will we not fear, though the earth do change, And though the mountains be moved in the heart of the seas; Though the waters thereof roar and be troubled, Though the mountains shake with the swelling thereof.

As they sang there came a noise as though the mountains really were shaking. The ground rocked; the walls shook; the chains were loosened from the stones; the stocks were wrenched apart; their hands and feet were free; the heavy doors crashed open. It was an earthquake.

The jailor leapt to the entrance of the prison. The moonlight shone on his sword as he was about to kill himself, thinking his prisoners had escaped.

"Do not harm yourself," shouted Paul. "We are all here."

"Torches! Torches!" yelled the jailor.

The jailor, like all the people of his land, believed that earthquakes were sent by God. He thought he was lost. He turned to Paul and Silas who, he knew, were teachers about God.

"Sirs," he said, falling in fear on the ground, "what must I do to be saved?"

"Believe in the Lord Jesus Christ," they replied, "and you and your household will all be saved."

The jailor's wife then brought some oil and water, and the jailor washed the poor wounded backs of Paul and Silas and rubbed healing oil into them.

The night was now passing and the sun began to rise. There was a tramp of feet. The lictors who had thrashed Paul and Silas marched to the door of the prison with an order to free them. The jailor was delighted.

"The priors have sent to set you free," he said. "Come out then and go in peace."

He had the greatest surprise in his life when, instead of going, Paul turned and said:

"No, indeed! The priors flogged us in public in the Forum and without a trial--flogged Roman citizens! They threw us publicly into prison, and now they are going to get rid of us secretly. Let the priors come here themselves and take us out!"

Surely it was the boldest message ever sent to the powerful priors. But Paul knew what he was doing, and when the Roman priors heard the message they knew that he was right. They would be ruined if it were reported at Rome that they had publicly flogged Roman citizens without trial.

Their prisoner, Paul, was now their judge. They climbed down from their marble seats and walked on foot to the prison to plead with Paul and Silas to leave the prison and not to tell against them what had happened.

"Will you go away from the city?" they asked. "We are afraid of other riots."

So Paul and Silas consented. But they went to the house where Lydia lived-- the home in which they had been staying in Philippi.

Paul cheered up the other Christian folk--Lydia and Luke and Timothy--and told them how the jailor and his wife and family had all become Christians.

"Keep the work of spreading the message here in Philippi going strongly," said Paul to Luke and Timothy. "Be cheerfully prepared for trouble." And then he and Silas, instead of going back to their own land, went out together in the morning light of the early winter of A.D. 50, away along the Western road over the hills to face perils in other cities in order to carry the Good News to the people of the West.

The Trail of the Hero-Scout.

So Paul the dauntless pioneer set his brave face westwards, following the long trail across the Roman Empire--the hero-scout of Christ. Nothing could stop him--not scourgings nor stonings, prison nor robbers, blizzards nor sand-storms. He went on and on till at last, as a prisoner in Rome, he laid his head on the block of the executioner and was slain. These are the brave words that we hear from him as he came near to the end:

+----------------------------+ | I HAVE FOUGHT A GOOD FIGHT; | | I HAVE RUN MY COURSE; | | I HAVE KEPT THE FAITH. | +----------------------------+

Long years afterward, men who were Christians in Rome carried the story of the Kingdom of Jesus Christ across Europe to some savages in the North Sea Islands--called Britons. Paul handed the torch from the Near East to the people in Rome. They passed the torch on to the people of Britain--and from Britain many years later men sailed to build up the new great nation in America. So the torch has run from East to West, from that day to this, and from those people of long ago to us. But we owe this most of all to Paul, the first missionary, who gave his life to bring the Good News from the lands of Syria and Judea, where our Lord Jesus Christ lived and died and rose again.

FOOTNOTES:

[Footnote 2: The dates are, of course, conjectural; but those given are accepted by high authorities. Paul was about forty-four at the time of this adventure.]

[Footnote 3: The plateau on which Lystra, Derbe, Iconium, and Antioch-in-Pisidia stood is from 3000 to 4000 feet above sea-level.]

[Footnote 4: The aqueduct was standing there in 1914, when the author was at Antioch-in-Pisidia (now called Yalowatch).]

[Footnote 5: A Bible with maps attached will give the route from Antioch in Syria, round the Gulf of Alexandretta, past Tarsus, up the Cilician Gates to Derbe, Lystra, Iconium, and Antioch-in-Pisidia.]

[Footnote 6: Compare Acts ix. I-8, xxvi. 12-20.]

[Footnote 7: St. Paul's motive and message are developed more fully in the Author's Paul the Dauntless.]

CHAPTER II

THE MEN OF THE SHINGLE BEACH

Wilfrid of Sussex (Date, born A.D. 634. Incidents A.D. 666 and 681[8])

Twelve hundred and fifty years ago a man named Wilfrid sailed along the south coast of a great island in the North Seas. With him in the ship were a hundred and twenty companions.

The voyage had started well, but now the captain looked anxious as he peered out under his curved hand, looking first south and then north. There was danger in both directions.

The breeze from the south stiffened to a gale. The mast creaked and strained as the gathering storm tore at the mainsail. The ship reeled and pitched as the spiteful waves smote her high bow and swept hissing and gurgling along the deck. She began to jib like a horse and refused to obey her rudder. Wind and current were carrying her out of her course.

In spite of all the captain's sea-craft the ship was being driven nearer to the dreaded, low, shingle beach of the island that stretched along the northern edge of the sea. The captain did not fear the coast itself, for it had no rocks. But the lines deepened on his weather-scarred face as he saw, gathering on the shelving beach, the wild, yellow-haired men of the island.

The ship was being carried nearer and nearer to the coast. All on board could now see the Men of the Shingle Beach waving their spears and axes.

The current and the wind swung the ship still closer to the shore, and now-- even above the whistle of the gale in the cordage--the crew heard the wild whoop of the wreckers. These men on the beach were the sons of pirates.

But they were now cowards compared with their fathers. For they no longer lived by the wild sea-rover's fight that had made their fathers' blood leap with the joy of the battle. They lived by a crueller craft. Waiting till some such vessel as this was swept ashore, they would swoop down on it, harry and slay the men, carry the women and children off for slaves, break up the ship and take the wood and stores for fire and food. They were beach-combers.

An extra swing of the tide, a great wave--and with a thud the ship was aground, stuck fast on the yielding sands. With a wild yell, and with their tawny manes streaming in the wind, the wreckers rushed down the beach brandishing their spears.

Wilfrid, striding to the side of the ship, raised his hand to show that he wished to speak to the chief. But the island men rushed on like an avalanche and started to storm the ship. Snatching up arms, poles, rope-ends--whatever they could find--the men on board beat down upon the heads of the savages as they climbed up the ship's slippery side. One man after another sank wounded on the deck. The fight grew more obstinate, but at last the men of the beach drew back up the sands, baffled.

The Men of the Shingle Beach might have given up the battle had not a fierce priest of their god of war leapt on to a mound of sand, and, lifting his naked arms to the skies, called on the god to destroy the men in the ship.

The savages were seized with a new frenzy and swept down the beach again. Wilfrid had gathered his closest friends round him and was quietly kneeling on the deck praying to his God for deliverance from the enemy. The fight became desperate. Again the savages were driven back up the beach.

Once more they rallied and came swooping down on the ship. But a pebble from the sling of a man on the ship struck the savage priest on the forehead; he tottered and fell on the sand. This infuriated the savages, yet it took the heart out of these men who had trusted in their god of war.

Meanwhile the tide had been creeping up; it swung in still further and lifted the ship from the sand; the wind veered, the sails strained. Slowly, but with gathering speed, the ship stood out to sea followed by howls of rage from the men on the beach.

* * * * *

Some years passed by, yet Wilfrid in all his travels had never forgotten the Men of the Beach. And, strangely enough, he wanted to go back to them.

At last the time came when he could do so. This time he did not visit them by sea. After he had preached among the people in a distant part of the same great island, Wilfrid with four faithful companions--Eappa, Padda, Burghelm and Oiddi--walked down to the south coast of the island.

As he came to the tribe he found many of them gathered on the beach as before. But the fierceness was gone. They tottered with weakness as they walked. The very bones seemed ready to come through their skin. They were starving with hunger and thirst from a long drought, when no grain or food of any kind would grow. And now they were gathered on the shore, and a long row of them linked hand in hand would rush down the very beach upon which they had attacked Wilfrid, and would cast themselves into the sea to get out of the awful agonies of their hunger.

"Are there not fish in the sea for food?" asked Wilfrid.

"Yes, but we cannot catch them," they answered.

Wilfrid showed the wondering Men of the Shingle Beach how to make large nets and then launched out in the little boats that they owned, and let the nets down. For hour after hour Wilfrid and his companions fished, while the savages watched them from the beach with hungry eyes as the silver-shining fish were drawn gleaming and struggling into the boats.

At last, as evening drew on, the nets were drawn in for the last time, and Wilfrid came back to the beach with hundreds of fish in the boats. With eager joy the Men of the Beach lit fires and cooked the fish. Their hunger was stayed; the rain for which Wilfrid prayed came. They were happy once more.

Then Wilfrid gathered them all around him on the beach and said words like these:

"You men tried to kill me and my friends on this beach years ago, trusting in your god of war. You failed. There is no god of war. There is but one God, a God not of war, but of Love, Who sent His only Son to tell about His love. That Son, Jesus Christ, Who fed the hungry multitudes by the side of the sea with fish, sent me to you to show love to you, feeding you with fish from the sea, and feeding you with His love, which is the Bread of Life."

The wondering savages, spear in hand, shook their matted hair and could not take it in at once. Yet they and their boys and girls had already learned to trust Wilfrid, and soon began to love the God of Whom he spoke.

* * * * *

Now, those savages were the great, great, great grandfathers and mothers of the English-speaking peoples of the world. The North Sea Island was Britain; the beach was at Selsey near Chichester on the South Coast. And the very fact that you and I are alive to-day, the shelter of our homes, the fact that we can enjoy the wind on the heath in camp, our books and sport and school, all these things come to us through men like Wilfrid and St. Patrick, St. Columba and St. Ninian, St. Augustine and others who in the days of long ago came to lift our fathers from the wretched, quarrelsome life, and from the starving helplessness of the Men of the Shingle Beach.

The people of the North Sea Islands and of America and the rest of the Christian world have these good things in their life because there came to save our forefathers heroic missionaries like Wilfrid, Columba, and Augustine. There are to-day men of the South Sea Islands, who are even more helpless than our Saxon grandfathers.

To get without giving is mean. To take the torch and not to pass it on is to fail to play the game. We must hand on to the others the light that has come to us.

FOOTNOTES:

[Footnote 8: The chief authority for the story of Wilfrid is Bede.]

CHAPTER III

THE KNIGHT OF A NEW CRUSADE

Raymund Lull (Dates, b. 1234, d. 1315)

I

A little old man, barefooted and bareheaded, and riding upon an ass, went through the cities and towns and villages of Europe, in the eleventh century, carrying--not a lance, but a crucifix. When he came near a town the word ran like a forest fire, "It is Peter the Hermit."

All the people rushed out. Their hearts burned as they heard him tell how the tomb of Jesus Christ was in the hand of the Moslem Turk, of how Christians going to worship at His Tomb in Jerusalem were thrown into prison and scourged and slain. Knights sold lands and houses to buy horses and lances. Peasants threw down the axe and the spade for the pike and bow and arrows. Led by knights, on whose armour a red Cross was emblazoned, the people poured out in their millions for the first Crusade. It is said that in the spring of 1096 an "expeditionary force" of six million people was heading toward Palestine.

The Crusades were caused partly by the cruelty of the followers of Mohammed, the Moslem Turks, who believed that they could earn entrance into Paradise by slaying infidel Christians. The Moslems every day and five times a day turn their faces to Mecca in Arabia, saying "There is no God but God; Mohammed is the Prophet of God." Allah (they believe) is wise and merciful to His own, but not holy, nor our Father, nor loving and forgiving, nor desiring pure lives. On earth and in Paradise women have no place save to serve men.

The first Crusade ended in the capture of Jerusalem (July 15, 1099), and Godfrey de Bouillon became King of Jerusalem. But Godfrey refused to put a crown upon his head. For, he said, "I will not wear a crown of gold in the city where Our Lord Jesus Christ wore a crown of thorns."

The fortunes of Christian and Moslem ebbed and flowed for nearly two hundred years, during which time there were seven Crusades ending at the fall of Acre into the hands of the Turks in 1291.

The way of the sword had failed, though indeed the Crusades had probably been the means of preventing all Europe from being overrun by the Moslems. At the time when the last Crusade had begun a man was planning a new kind of Crusade, different in method but calling for just as much bravery as the old kind. We are going to hear his story now.

II

The Young Knight's Vision

In the far-off days of the last of the Crusades, a knight of Majorca, in the Mediterranean Sea, stood on the shore of his island home gazing over the water. Raymund Lull from the beach of Palma Bay, where he had played as a boy, now looked out southward, where boats with their tall, rakish, brown sails ran in from the Great Sea.

The knight was dreaming of Africa which lay away to the south of his island. He had heard many strange stories from the sailors about the life in the harbours of that mysterious African seaboard; but he had never once in his thirty-six years set eyes upon one of its ports.

It was the year when Prince Edward of England, out on the mad, futile adventure of the last Crusade, was felled by the poisoned dagger of an assassin in Nazareth, and when Eleanor (we are told) drew the poison from the wound with her own lips. Yet Raymund Lull, who was a knight so skilled that he could flash his sword and set his lance in rest with any of his peers, had not joined that Crusade. His brave father carried the scars of a dozen battles against the Moors. Yet, when the last Crusade swept down the Mediterranean, Lull stood aside; for he was himself planning a new Crusade of a kind unlike any that had gone before.

He dreamed of a Crusade not to the Holy Land but to Africa, where the Crescent of Mohammed ruled and where the Cross of Christ was never seen save when an arrogant Moslem drew a cross in the sand of the desert to spit upon it. It was the desire of Raymund Lull's life to sail out into those perilous ports and to face the fierce Saracens who thronged the cities. He longed for this as other knights panted to go out to the Holy Land as Crusaders. He was rich enough to sail at any time, for he was his own master. Why, then, did he not take one of the swift craft that rocked in the bay, and sail?

It was because he had not yet forged a sharp enough weapon for his new Crusade. His deep resolve was that at all costs he would "Be Prepared" for every counter-stroke of the Saracen whose tongue was as swift and sharp as his scimitar.

What powers do we think a man should have in order to convince fanatical Moslems, who knew their own sacred book--the Koran--of the truth of Christianity? Control of his own temper, courage, patience, knowledge of the Moslem religion and of the Bible, suggest themselves.

III

The Preparation of Temper So Lull turned his back on the beach and on Africa, and plunged under the heavy shadows of the arched gateway through the city wall up the narrow streets of Palma. A servant opened the heavy, studded door of his father's mansion--the house where Lull himself was born.

He hastened in and, calling to his Saracen slave, strode to his own room. The dark-faced Moor obediently came, bowed before his young master, and laid out on the table manuscripts that were covered with mysterious writing such as few people in Europe could read.

Lull was learning Arabic from this sullen Saracen slave. He was studying the Koran--the Bible of the Mohammedans--so that he might be able to strive with the Saracens on their own ground. For Lull knew that he must be master of all the knowledge of the Moslem if he was to win his battles; just as a knight in the fighting Crusades must be swift and sure with his sword. And this is how Lull spoke of the Crusade on which he was to set out.

"I see many knights," he said, "going to the Holy Land beyond the seas and thinking that they can acquire it by force of arms; but in the end all are destroyed before they attain that which they think to have. Whence it seems to me that the conquest of the Holy Land ought not to be attempted except in the way in which Christ and His Apostles achieved it, namely, by love and prayers, and the pouring out of tears and blood."

Suddenly, as he and the Saracen slave argued together, the Moor blurted out passionately a horrible blasphemy against the name of Jesus. Lull's blood was up. He leapt to his feet, leaned forward, and caught the Moor a swinging blow on the face with his hand. In a fury the Saracen snatched a dagger from the folds of his robe and, leaping at Lull, drove it into his side. Raymund fell with a cry. Friends rushed in. The Saracen was seized and hurried away to a prison-cell, where he slew himself.

Lull, as he lay day after day waiting for his wound to heal and remembering his wild blow at the Saracen, realised that, although he had learned Arabic, he had not yet learned the first lesson of his own new way of Crusading--to be master of himself.

IV

The Preparation of Courage So Raymund Lull (at home and in Rome and Paris) set himself afresh to his task of preparing. At last he felt that he was ready. From Paris he rode south-east through forest and across plain, over mountain and pass, till the gorgeous palaces and the thousand masts of Genoa came in sight.

He went down to the harbour and found a ship that was sailing across the Mediterranean to Africa. He booked his passage and sent his goods with all his precious manuscripts aboard. The day for sailing came. His friends came to cheer him. But Lull sat in his room trembling.

As he covered his eyes with his hands in shame, he saw the fiery, persecuting Saracens of Tunis, whom he was sailing to meet. He knew they were glowing with pride because of their triumphs over the Crusaders in Palestine. He knew they were blazing with anger because their brother Moors had been slaughtered and tortured in Spain. He saw ahead of him the rack, the thumb-screw, and the boot; the long years in a slimy dungeon--at the best the executioner's scimitar. He simply dared not go.

The books were brought ashore again. The ship sailed without Lull.

"The ship has gone," said a friend to Lull. He quivered under a torture of shame greater than the agony of the rack. He was wrung with bitter shame that he who had for all these years prepared for this Crusade should now have shown the white feather. He was, indeed, a craven knight of Christ.

His agony of spirit threw him into a high fever that kept him in his bed.

Soon after he heard that another ship was sailing for Africa.

In spite of the protestations of his friends Lull insisted that they should carry him to the ship. They did so; but as the hour of sailing drew on his friends were sure that he was so weak that he would die on the sea before he could reach Africa. So--this time in spite of all his pleading--they carried him ashore again. But he could not rest and his agony of mind made his fever worse.

Soon, however, a third ship was making ready to sail. This time Lull was carried on board and refused to return.

The ship cast off and threaded its way through the shipping of the harbour out into the open sea.

"From this moment," said Lull, "I was a new man. All fever left me almost before we were out of sight of land."

V

The First Battle Passing Corsica and Sardinia, the ship slipped southward till at last she made the yellow coast of Africa, broken by the glorious Gulf of Tunis. She dropped sail as she ran alongside the busy wharves of Goletta. Lull was soon gliding in a boat through the short ancient canal to Tunis, the mighty city which was head of all the Western Mohammedan world.

He landed and found the place beside the great mosque where the grey-bearded scholars bowed over their Korans and spoke to one another about the law of Mohammed.

They looked at him with amazement as he boldly came up to them and said, "I have come to talk with you about Christ and His Way of Life, and

Mohammed and his teaching. If you can prove to me that Mohammed is indeed the Prophet, I will myself become a follower of him."

The Moslems, sure of their case, called together their wisest men and together they declaimed to Lull what he already knew very well--the watchword that rang out from minaret to minaret across the roofs of the vast city as the first flush of dawn came up from the East across the Gulf. "There is no God but God; Mohammed is the Prophet of God."

"Yes," he replied, "the Allah of Mohammed is one and is great, but He does not love as does the Father of Jesus Christ. He is wise, but He does not do good to men like our God who so loved the world that He gave His Son Jesus Christ."

To and fro the argument swung till, after many days, to their dismay and amazement the Moslems saw some of their number waver and at last actually beginning to go over to the side of Lull. To forsake the Faith of Mohammed is--by their own law--to be worthy of death. A Moslem leader hurried to the Sultan of Tunis.

"See," he said, "this learned teacher, Lull, is declaring the errors of the Faith. He is dangerous. Let us take him and put him to death."

The Sultan gave the word of command. A body of soldiers went out, seized Lull, dragged him through the streets, and threw him into a dark dungeon to wait the death sentence.

But another Moslem who had been deeply touched by Lull's teaching craved audience with the Sultan.

"See," he said, "this learned man Lull--if he were a Moslem--would be held in high honour, being so brave and fearless in defence of his Faith. Do not slay him. Banish him from Tunis."

So when Lull in his dungeon saw the door flung open and waited to be taken to his death he found to his surprise that he was led from the dungeon through the streets of Tunis, taken along the canal, thrust into the hold of a ship, and told that he must go in that ship to Genoa and never return. But the man who had before been afraid to sail from Genoa to Tunis, now escaped unseen from the ship that would have taken him back to safety in order to risk his life once more. He said to himself the motto he had written:

```
+---------------------------------------+ | "HE WHO LOVES NOT, LIVES NOT! HE WHO
| | LIVES BY THE LIFE CANNOT DIE." | +---------------------------------------+
```

He was not afraid now even of martyrdom. He hid among the wharves and gathered his converts about him to teach them more and more about Christ.

VI

The Last Fight At last, however, seeing that he could do little in hiding, Lull took ship to Naples. After many adventures during a number of years, in a score of cities and on the seas, the now white-haired Lull sailed into the curved bay of Bugia farther westward along the African coast. In the bay behind the frowning walls the city with its glittering mosques climbed the hill. Behind rose two glorious mountains crowned with the dark green of the cedar. And, far off, like giant Moors wearing white turbans, rose the distant mountain peaks crowned with snow.

Lull passed quietly through the arch of the city gateway which he knew so well, for among other adventures he had once been imprisoned in this very city. He climbed the steep street and found a friend who hid him away. There for a year Lull taught in secret till he felt that the time had come for him to go out boldly and dare death itself.

One day the people in the market-place of Bugia heard a voice ring out that seemed to some of them strangely familiar. They hurried toward the sound. There stood the old hero with arm uplifted declaring, in the full blaze of the North African day, the Love of God shown in Jesus Christ His Son.

The Saracens murmured. They could not answer his arguments. They cried to him to stop, but his voice rose ever fuller and bolder. They rushed on him, dragged him by the cloak out of the market-place, down the streets, under the archway to a place beyond the city walls. There they threw back their sleeves, took up great jagged stones and hurled these grim messengers of hate at the Apostle of Love, till he sank senseless to the ground.[9]

It was word for word over again the story of Stephen; the speech, the wild cries of the mob, the rush to the place beyond the city wall, the stoning.[10]

Did Lull accomplish anything? He was dead; but he had conquered. He had conquered his old self. For the Lull who had, in a fit of temper, smitten his Saracen slave now smiled on the men who stoned him; and the Lull who had showed the white feather of fear at Genoa, now defied death in the market-place of Bugia. And in that love and heroism, in face of hate and death, he had shown men the only way to conquer the scimitar of Mohammed, "the way in which Christ and His Apostles achieved it, namely, by love and prayers, and the pouring out of tears and blood."

FOOTNOTES:

[Footnote 9: June 30. 1315.]

[Footnote 10: Acts vi. 8-vii. 60.]

CHAPTER IV

FRANCIS COEUR-DE-LION

(_St. Francis of Assisi_) A.D. 1181-1226 (Date of Incident, 1219)

I

The dark blue sky of an Italian night was studded with sparkling stars that seemed to be twinkling with laughter at the pranks of a lively group of gay young fellows as they came out from a house half-way up the steep street of the little city of Assisi.

As they strayed together down the street they sang the love-songs of their country and then a rich, strong voice rang out singing a song in French.

"That is Francis Bernardone," one neighbour would say to another, nodding his head, for Francis could sing, not only in his native Italian, but also in French.

"He lives like a prince; yet he is but the son of a cloth merchant,--rich though the merchant be."

So the neighbours, we are told, were always grumbling about Francis, the wild spendthrift. For young Francis dressed in silk and always in the latest fashion; he threw his pocket-money about with a free hand. He loved beautiful things. He was very sensitive. He would ride a long way round to avoid seeing the dreadful face of a poor leper, and would hold his nose in his cloak as he passed the place where the lepers lived.

He was handsome in face, gallant in bearing, idle and careless; a jolly companion, with beautiful courtly manners. His dark chestnut hair curled over his smooth, rather small forehead. His black twinkling eyes looked out under level brows; his nose was straight and finely shaped.

When he laughed he showed even, white, closely set teeth between thin and sensitive lips. He wore a short, black beard. His arms were shortish; his fingers long and sensitive. He was lightly built; his skin was delicate.

He was witty, and his voice when he spoke was powerful and sonorous, yet sweet-toned and very clear.

For him to be the son of a merchant seemed to the gossips of Assisi all wrong--as though a grey goose had hatched out a gorgeous peacock.

The song of the revellers passed down the street and died away. The little city of Assisi slept in quietness on the slopes of the Apennine Mountains under the dark clear sky.

A few nights later, however, no song of any revellers was heard. Francis Bernardone was very ill with a fever. For week after week his mother nursed him; and each night hardly believed that her son would live to see the light of the next morning. When at last the fever left him, he was so feeble that for weeks he could not rise from his bed. Gradually, however, he got better: as he did so the thing that he desired most of all in the world was to see the lovely country around Assisi;--the mountains, the Umbrian Plain beneath, the blue skies, the dainty flowers.

At last one day, with aching limbs and in great feebleness, he crept out of doors. There were the great Apennine Mountains on the side of which his city of Assisi was built. There were the grand rocky peaks pointing to the intense blue sky. There was the steep street with the houses built of stone of a strange, delicate pink colour, as though the light of dawn were always on them. There were the dark green olive trees, and the lovely tendrils of the vines. The gay Italian flowers were blooming.

Stretching away in the distance was one of the most beautiful landscapes of the world; the broad Umbrian Plain with its browns and greens melting in the distance into a bluish haze that softened the lines of the distant hills.

How he had looked forward to seeing it all, to being in the sunshine, to feeling the breeze on his hot brow! But what--he wondered--had happened to him? He looked at it all, but he felt no joy. It all seemed dead and empty. He turned his back on it and crawled indoors again, sad and sick at heart. He was sure that he would never feel again "the wild joys of living."

As Francis went back to his bed he began to think what he should do with the rest of his life. He made up his mind not to waste it any longer: but he did not see clearly what he should do with it.

A short time after Francis begged a young nobleman of Assisi, who was just starting to fight in a war, if he might go with him. The nobleman--Walter of Brienne, agreed: so Francis bought splendid trappings for his horse, and a shield, sword and spear. His armour and his horse's harness were more splendid than even those of Walter. So they went clattering together out of Assisi.

But he had not gone thirty miles before he was smitten again by fever. After sunset one evening he lay dreamily on his bed when he seemed to hear a voice.

"Francis," it asked, "what could benefit thee most, the master or the servant, the rich man or the poor?"

"The master and the rich man," answered Francis in surprise.

"Why then," went on the voice, "dost thou leave God, Who is the Master and rich, for man, who is the servant and poor?"

"Then, Lord, what will Thou that I do?" asked Francis.

"Return to thy native town, and it shall be shown thee there what thou shall do," said the voice.

He obediently rose and went back to Assisi. He tried to join again in the old revels, but the joy was gone. He went quietly away to a cave on the mountain side and there he lay--as young Mahomet had done, you remember, five centuries before, to wonder what he was to do.

Then a vision came to him. All at once like a flash his mind was clear, and his soul was full of joy. He saw the love of Jesus Christ--Who had lived and suffered and died for love of him and of all men;--that love was to rule his own life! He had found his Captain--the Master of his life, the Lord of his service,--Christ.

Yet even now he hardly knew what to do. He went home and told his friends as well as he could of the change in his heart.

Some smiled rather pityingly and went away saying to one another: "Poor fellow; a little mad, you can see; very sad for his parents!"

Others simply laughed and mocked.

One day, very lonely and sad at heart, he clambered up the mountain side to an old church just falling into ruin near which, in a cavern, lived a priest. He went into the ruin and fell on his knees.

"Francis," a voice in his soul seemed to say, "dost thou see my house going to ruin. Buckle to and repair it."

He dashed home, saddled his horse, loaded it with rich garments and rode off to another town to sell the goods. He sold the horse too; trudged back up the hill and gave the fat purse to the priest.

"No," said the priest, "I dare not take it unless your father says I may."

But his father, who had got rumour of what was going on, came with a band of friends to drag Francis home. Francis fled through the woods to a secret cave, where he lay hidden till at last he made up his mind to face all. He came out and walked straight towards home. Soon the townsmen of Assisi caught sight of him.

"A madman," they yelled, throwing stones and sticks at him. All the boys of Assisi came out and hooted and threw pebbles.

His father heard the riot and rushed out to join in the fun. Imagine his horror when he found that it was his own son. He yelled with rage, dashed at him and, clutching him by the robe, dragged him along, beating and cursing him. When he got him home he locked him up. But some days later Francis' mother let him out, when his father was absent; and Francis climbed the hill to the Church.

The bishop called in Francis and his father to his court to settle the quarrel.

"You must give back to your father all that you have," said he.

"I will," replied Francis.

He took off all his rich garments; and, clad only in a hair-vest, he put the clothes and the purse of money at his father's feet.

"Now," he cried, "I have but one father. Henceforth I can say in all truth 'Our Father Who art in heaven.'"

A peasant's cloak was given to Francis. He went thus, without home or any money, a wanderer. He went to a monastery and slaved in the kitchen. A friend gave him a tunic, some shoes, and a stick. He went out wandering in Italy again. He loved everybody; he owned nothing; he wanted everyone to know the love of Jesus as he knew and enjoyed that love.

There came to Francis many adventures. He was full of joy; he sang even to the birds in the woods. Many men joined him as his disciples in the way of obedience, of poverty, and of love. Men in Italy, in Spain, in Germany and in Britain caught fire from the flame of his simple love and careless courage. Never had Europe seen so clear a vision of the love of Jesus. His followers were called the Lesser Brothers (Friars Minor).

All who can should read the story of Francis' life: as for us we are here going simply to listen to what happened to him on a strange and perilous adventure.

II

About this time people all over Europe were agog with excitement about the Crusades. Four Crusades had come and gone. Richard Coeur-de-Lion was dead. But the passion for fighting against the Saracen was still in the hearts of men.

"The tomb of our Lord in Jerusalem is in the hands of the Saracen," the cry went up over all Europe. "Followers of Jesus Christ are slain by the scimitars of Islam. Let us go and wrest the Holy City from the hands of the Saracen."

There was also the danger to Europe itself. The Mohammedans ruled in Spain as well as in North Africa, in Egypt and in the Holy Land.

So rich men sold their lands to buy horses and armour and to fit themselves and their foot soldiers for the fray. Poor men came armed with pike and helmet and leather jerkin. The knights wore a blood-red cross on their white tunics. In thousands upon thousands, with John of Brienne as their Commander-in-Chief (the brother of that Walter of Brienne with whom, you remember, Francis had started for the wars as a knight), they sailed the Mediterranean to fight for the Cross in Egypt.

They attacked Egypt because the Sultan there ruled over Jerusalem and they hoped by defeating him to free Jerusalem at the same time.

As Francis saw the knights going off to the Crusades in shining armour with the trappings of their horses all a-glitter and a-jingle, and as he thought of the lands where the people worshipped--not the God and Father of our Lord Jesus Christ--but the "Sultan in the Sky," the Allah of Mahomet, his spirit caught fire within him.

Francis had been a soldier and a knight only a few years before. He could not but feel the stir of the Holy War in his veins,--the tingle of the desire to be in it. He heard the stories of the daring of the Crusaders; he heard of a great victory over the Saracens.

Francis, indeed, wanted Jesus Christ to conquer men more than he wanted anything on earth; but he knew that men are only conquered by Jesus Christ if their hearts are changed by Him.

"Even if the Saracens are put to the sword and overwhelmed, still they are not saved," he said to himself.

As he thought these things he felt sure that he heard them calling to him (as the Man from Macedonia had called to St. Paul)--"Come over and help us." St. Paul had brought the story of Jesus Christ to Europe; and had suffered prison and scourging and at last death by the executioner's sword in doing it; must not Francis be ready to take the same message back again from Europe to the Near East and to suffer for it?

"I will go," he said, "but to save the Saracens, not to slay them."

He was not going out to fight, yet he had in his heart a plan that needed him to be braver and more full of resource than any warrior in the armies of the Crusades. He was as much a Lion-hearted hero as Richard Coeur-de-Lion himself, and was far wiser and indeed more powerful.

So he took a close friend, Brother Illuminato, with him and they sailed away together over the seas. They sailed from Italy with Walter of Brienne, with one of the Crusading contingents in many ships. Southeast they voyaged over the blue waters of the Mediterranean Sea.

Francis talked with the Crusaders on board; and much that they said and did made him very sad. They squabbled with one another. The knights were arrogant and sneered at the foot soldiers; the men-at-arms did not trust the knights. They had the Cross on their armour; but few of them had in their hearts the spirit of Jesus who was nailed to the Cross.

At last the long, yellow coast-line of Egypt was sighted. Behind it lay the minarets and white roofs of a city. They were come to the eastern mouth of the Nile, on which stood the proud city of Damietta. The hot rays of the sun smote down upon the army of the Crusaders as they landed. The sky and the sea were of an intense blue; the sand and the sun glared at one another.

Francis would just be able to hear at dawn the cry of the muezzin from the minarets of Damietta, "Come to prayer: there is no God but Allah and Mahomet is his prophet. Come to prayer. Prayer is better than sleep."

John of Brienne began to muster his men in battle array to attack the Sultan of Egypt, Malek-Kamel, a name which means "the Perfect Prince."

Francis, however, was quite certain that the attempt would be a ghastly failure. He hardly knew what to do. So he talked it over with his friend, Brother Illuminato.

"I know they will be defeated in this attempt," he said. "But if I tell them so they will treat me as a madman. On the other hand, if I do not tell them, then my conscience will condemn me. What do you think I ought to do?"

"My brother," said Illuminate, "what does the judgment of the world matter to you? If they say you are mad it will not be the first time!"

Francis, therefore, went to the Crusaders and warned them. They laughed scornfully. The order for advance was given. The Crusaders charged into battle. Francis was in anguish--tears filled his eyes. The Saracens came out and fell upon the Christian soldiers and slaughtered them. Over 6000 of them either fell under the scimitar or were taken prisoner. The Crusaders were defeated.

Francis' mind was now fully made up. He went to a Cardinal, who represented the Pope, with the Crusading Army to ask his leave to go and preach to the Sultan of Egypt.

"No," said the Cardinal, "I cannot give you leave to go. I know full well that you would never escape to come back alive. The Sultan of Egypt has offered a reward of gold to any man who will bring to him the head of a Christian. That will be your fate."

"Do suffer us to go, we do not fear death," pleaded Francis and Illuminato, again and again.

"I do not know what is in your minds in this," said the Cardinal, "but beware--if you go--that your thoughts are always to God."

"We only wish to go for great good, if we can work it," replied Francis.

"Then if you wish it so much," the Cardinal at last agreed, "you may go."

So Francis and Illuminato girded their loins and tightened their sandals and set away from the Crusading Army towards the very camp of the enemy.

As he walked Francis sang with his full, loud, clear voice. These were the words that he sang:

Yea though I walk through the valley of the shadow of death, I will fear no evil; for thou art with me; Thy rod and thy staff, they comfort me.

As they walked along over the sandy waste they saw two small sheep nibbling the sparse grass growing near the Nile.

"Be of good cheer," said Francis to Illuminato, smiling, "it is the fulfilling of the Gospel words 'Behold I send you as sheep in the midst of wolves.'"

Then there appeared some Saracen soldiers. They were, at first, for letting the two unarmed men go by; but, on questioning Francis, they grew angrier and angrier.

"Are you deserters from the Christian camp?" they asked.

"No," replied Francis.

"Are you envoys from the commander come to plead for peace?"

"No," was the answer again.

"Will you give up the infidel religion and become a true believer and say 'There is no God but Allah, and Mahomet is his prophet?'"

"No, no," cried Francis, "we are come to preach the Good News of Jesus Christ to the Sultan of Egypt."

The eyes of the Saracen soldiers opened with amazement: they could hardly believe their ears. Their faces flushed under their dark skins with anger.

"Chain them," they cried to one another. "Beat them--the infidels."

Chains were brought and snapped upon the wrists and ankles of Francis and Illuminato. Then they took rods and began to beat the two men--just as Paul and Silas had been beaten eleven centuries earlier.

As the rods whistled through the air and came slashing upon their wounded backs Francis kept crying out one word--"Soldan--Soldan." That is "Sultan--Sultan."

He thus made them understand that he wished to be taken to their Commander-in-Chief. So they decided to take these strange beings to Malek-Kamel.

As the Sultan sat in his pavilion Francis and Illuminato were led in. They bowed and saluted him courteously and Malek-Kamel returned the salute.

"Have you come with a message from your Commander?" said the Sultan.

"No," replied Francis.

"You wish then to become Saracens--worshippers of Allah in the name of Mahomet?"

"Nay, nay," answered Francis, "Saracens we will never be. We have come with a message from God; it is a message that will save your life. If you die under the law of Mahomet you are lost. We have come to tell you so: if you listen to us we will show all this to you."

The Sultan seems to have been amused and interested rather than angry.

"I have bishops and archbishops of my own," he said, "they can tell me all that I wish to know."

"Of this we are glad," replied Francis, "send and fetch them, if you will."

The Sultan agreed; he sent for eight of his Moslem great men. When they came in he said to them: "See these men, they have come to teach us a new faith. Shall we listen to them?"

"Sire," they answered him at once, "thou knowest the law: thou art bound to uphold it and carry it out. By Mahomet who gave us the law to slay infidels, we command thee that their heads be cut off. We will not listen to a word that they say. Off with their heads!"

The great men, having given their judgment, solemnly left the presence of the Sultan. The Sultan turned to Francis and Illuminato.

"Masters," he said to them, "they have commanded me by Mahomet to have your heads cut off. But I will go against the law, for you have risked your lives to save my immortal soul. Now leave me for the time."

The two Christian missionaries were led away; but in a day or two Malek-Kamel called them to his presence again.

"If you will stay in my dominions," he said, "I will give you land and other possessions."

"Yes," said Francis, "I will stay--on one condition--that you and your people turn to the worship of the true God. See," he went on, "let us put it to the test. Your priests here," and he pointed to some who were standing about, "they will not let me talk with them; will they do something. Have a great fire lighted. I will walk into the fire with them: the result will shew you whose faith is the true one."

As Francis suggested this idea the faces of the Moslem leaders were transfigured with horror. They turned and quietly walked away.

"I do not think," said the Sultan with a sarcastic smile at their retreating backs, "that any of my priests are ready to face the flames to defend their faith."

"Well, I will go alone into the fire," said Francis. "If I am burned--it is because of my sins--if I am protected by God then you will own Him as your God."

"No," replied the Sultan, "I will not listen to the idea of such a trial of your life for my soul." But he was astonished beyond measure at the amazing faith of Francis. So Francis withdrew from the presence of the Sultan, who at once sent after him rich and costly presents.

"You must take them back," said Francis to the messengers; "I will not take them."

"Take them to build your churches and support your priests," said the Sultan through his messengers.

But Francis would not take any gift from the Sultan. He left him and went back with Illuminato from the Saracen host to the camp of the Crusaders. As he was leaving the Sultan secretly spoke with Francis and said: "Will you pray for me that I may be guided by an inspiration from above that I may join myself to the religion that is most approved by God?"

The Sultan told off a band of his soldiers to go with the two men and to protect them from any molesting till they reached the Crusaders' Camp. There is a legend--though no one now can tell whether it is true or not--that when the Sultan of Egypt lay dying he sent for a disciple of Francis to be with him and pray for him. Whether this was so or not, it is quite clear that Francis had left in the memory of the Sultan such a vision of dauntless faith as he had never seen before or was ever to see again.

The Crusaders failed to win Egypt or the Holy Land; but to-day men are going from America and Britain in the footsteps of Francis of Assisi the Christian missionary, to carry to the people in Egypt, in the Holy Land and in all the Near East, the message that Francis took of the love of Jesus Christ. The stories of some of the deeds they have done and are to-day doing, we shall read in later chapters in this book.

Book Two: THE ISLAND ADVENTURERS

CHAPTER V

THE ADVENTUROUS SHIP

The Duff (Date of Incident, 1796)

A ship crept quietly down the River Thames on an ebb-tide. She was slipping out from the river into the estuary when suddenly a challenge rang out across the grey water.

"What ship is that?"

"The Duff," was the answer that came back from the little ship whose captain had passed through a hundred hairsbreadth escapes in his life but was now starting on the strangest adventure of them all.

"Whither bound?" came the challenge again from the man-o'-war that had hailed them.

"Otaheite," came the answer, which would startle the Government officer. For Tahiti[11] (as we now call it) was many thousands of miles away in the heart of the South Pacific Ocean. Indeed it had only been discovered by Captain Cook twenty-eight years earlier in 1768. The Duff was a small sailing-ship such as one of our American ocean liners of to-day could put into her dining saloon.

"What cargo?" The question came again from the officer on the man-o'-war.

"Missionaries and provisions," was Captain Wilson's answer.

The man-o'-war's captain was puzzled. He did not know what strange beings might be meant by missionaries. He was suspicious. Were they pirates, perhaps, in disguise!

We can understand how curious it would sound to him when we remember that (although Wilfrid and Augustine and Columba had gone to Britain as missionaries over a thousand years before The Duff started down the Thames) no cargo of missionaries had ever before sailed from those North Sea Islands of Britain to the savages of other lands like the South Sea Islands.

There was a hurried order and a scurry on board the Government ship. A boat was let down into the Thames, and half a dozen sailors tumbled into her and rowed to _The Duff._ What did the officer find?

He was met at the rail by a man who had been through scores of adventures, Captain Wilson. The son of the captain of a Newcastle collier, Wilson had grown up a dare-devil sailor boy. He enlisted as a soldier in the American war, became captain of a vessel trading with India, and was then captured and imprisoned by the French in India. He escaped from prison by climbing a great wall, and dropping down forty feet on the other side. He plunged into a river full of alligators, and swam across, escaping the jaws of alligators only to be captured on the other bank by Indians, chained and made to march barefoot for 500 miles. Then he was thrust into Hyder Ali's loathsome prison, starved and loaded with irons, and at last at the end of two years was set free.

This was the daring hero who had now undertaken to captain the little Duff across the oceans of the world to the South Seas. With Captain Wilson, the man-o'-war officer found also six carpenters, two shoemakers, two bricklayers, two sailors, two smiths, two weavers, a surgeon, a hatter, a shopkeeper, a cotton factor, a cabinet-maker, a draper, a harness maker, a tin worker, a butcher and four ministers. But they were all of them missionaries. With them were six children.

All up and down the English Channel French frigates sailed like hawks waiting to pounce upon their prey; for England was at war with France in those days. So for five weary weeks The Duff anchored in the roadstead of Spithead till, as one of a fleet of fifty-seven vessels, she could sail down the channel and across the Bay of Biscay protected by British men-o'-war. Safely clear of the French cruisers, The Duff held on alone till the cloud-capped mountain-heights of Madeira hove in sight.

Across the Atlantic she stood, for the intention was to sail round South America into the Pacific. But on trying to round the Cape Horn The Duff met such violent gales that Captain Wilson turned her in her tracks and headed back across the Atlantic for the Cape of Good Hope.

Week after week for thousands and thousands of miles she sailed. She had travelled from Rio de Janiero over 10,000 miles and had only sighted a single sail--a longer journey than any ship had ever sailed without seeing land.

"Shall we see the island to-day?" the boys on board would ask Captain Wilson. Day after day he shook his head. But one night he said:

"If the wind holds good to-night we shall see an island in the morning, but not the island where we shall stop."

"Land ho!" shouted a sailor from the masthead in the morning, and, sure enough, they saw away on the horizon, like a cloud on the edge of the sea, the island of Toobonai.[12]

As they passed Toobonai the wind rose and howled through the rigging. It tore at the sail of _The Duff,_ and the great Pacific waves rolled swiftly by, rushing and hissing along the sides of the little ship and tossing her on their foaming crests. But she weathered the storm, and, as the wind dropped, and they looked ahead, they saw, cutting into the sky-line, the mountain tops of Tahiti.

It was Saturday night when the island came in sight. Early on the Sunday morning by seven o'clock The Duff swung round under a gentle breeze into Matavai[13] Bay and dropped anchor. But before she could even anchor the whole bay had become alive with Tahitians. They thronged the beach, and, leaping into canoes, sent them skimming across the bay to the ship.

Captain Wilson, scanning the canoes swiftly and anxiously, saw with relief that the men were not armed. But the missionaries were startled when the savages climbed up the sides of the ship, and with wondering eyes rolling in their wild heads peered over the rail of the deck. They then leapt on board and began dancing like mad on the deck with their bare feet. From the canoes the Tahitians hauled up pigs, fowl, fish, bananas, and held them for the white men to buy. But Captain Wilson and all his company would not buy on that day--for it was Sunday.

The missionaries gathered together on deck to hold their Sunday morning service. The Tahitians stopped dancing and looked on with amazement, as the company of white men with their children knelt to pray and then read from the Bible.

The Tahitians could not understand this strange worship, with no god that could be seen. But when the white fathers and mothers and children sang, the savages stood around with wonder and delight on their faces as they listened to the strange and beautiful sounds.

But the startling events of the day were not over. For out from the beach came a canoe across the bay, and in it two Swedish sailors, named, like some fishermen of long ago, Peter and Andrew. These white men knew some English, but lived, not as Christians, but as the natives lived.

And after them came a great and aged chief named Haamanemane.[14] This great chief went up to the "chief" of the ship, Captain Wilson, and called out to him "Taio."[15]

They did not know what this meant, till Peter the Swede explained that Haamanemane wished to be the brother--the troth-friend of Captain Wilson. They were even to change names. Captain Wilson would be called Haamanemane, and Haamanemane would be called Wilson.

So Captain Wilson said "Taio," and he and the chief, who was also high priest of the gods of Tahiti, were brothers.

Captain Wilson said to Haamanemane, through Peter, who translated each to the other:

"We wish to come and live in this island."

Haamanemane said that he would speak to the king and queen of Tahiti about it. So he got down again over the side of the vessel into the canoe, and the paddles of his boatman flashed as they swept along over the breakers to the beach to tell the king of the great white chief who had come to visit them.

All these things happened on the Sunday. On Tuesday word came that the king and the queen would receive them. So Captain Wilson and all his missionaries got into the whale-boat and pulled for the shore. The natives rushed into the water, seized the boat and hauled her aground out of reach of the great waves.

They were startled to see the king and queen come riding on the shoulders of men. Even when one bearer grew tired and the king or the queen must get upon another, they were not allowed to touch the ground. The reason was that all the land they touched became their own, and the people carried them about so that they themselves might not lose their land and houses by the king and queen touching them.

So at that place, under the palm trees of Tahiti, with the beating of the surf on the shore before them, and the great mountain forests behind, these brown islanders of the South Seas gave a part of their land to Captain Wilson and his men that they might live there.

The sons of the wild men of the North Sea Islands had met their first great adventure in bringing to the men of the South Sea Islands the story of the love of the Father of all.

FOOTNOTES:

[Footnote 11: Ta-hee-tee.]

[Footnote 12: Too-b[=o]-n[=a]-ee.]

[Footnote 13: M[=a]-t[)a]-v[)a]-ee.]

[Footnote 14: Haa-m[)u]-n[=a]y-m[)a]-n.]

[Footnote 15: Ta-ce-[=o].]

CHAPTER VI

THE ISLAND BEACON FIRES

Papeiha[16]

(Date of Incident, 1823)

The edge of the sea was just beginning to gleam with the gold of the rising sun. The captain of a little ship, that tossed and rolled on the tumbling ocean, looked out anxiously over the bow. Around him everywhere was the wild waste of the Pacific Ocean. Through day after day he had tacked and veered, baffled by contrary winds. Now, with little food left in the ship, starvation on the open ocean stared them in the face.

They were searching for an island of which they had heard, but which they had never seen.

The captain searched the horizon again, but he saw nothing, except that ahead of him, on the sky-line to the S.W., great clouds had gathered. He turned round and went to the master-missionary--the hero and explorer and shipbuilder, John Williams, saying:

"We must give up the search or we shall all be starved."

John Williams knew that this was true; yet he hated the thought of going back. He was a scout exploring at the head of God's navy. He had left his home in London and with his young wife had sailed across the world to the South Seas to carry the Gospel of Jesus Christ to the people there. He was living on the island of Raiatea: but as he himself said, "I cannot be confined within the limits of a single reef." He wanted to pass on the torch to other islands. So he was now on this voyage of discovery.

It was seven o'clock when the captain told John Williams that they must give up the search.

"In an hour's time," said Williams, "we will turn back if we have not sighted Rarotonga."

So they sailed on. The sun climbed the sky, the cool dawn was giving way to the heat of day.

"Go up the mast and look ahead," said Williams to a South Sea Island native. Then he paced the deck, hoping to hear the cry of "Land," but nothing could the native see.

"Go up again," cried Williams a little later. And again there was nothing. Four times the man climbed the mast, and four times he reported only sea and sky and cloud. Gradually the sun's heat had gathered up the great mountains of cloud, and the sky was clear to the edge of the ocean. Then there came a sudden cry from the masthead:

"Teie teie, taua fenua, nei!"[17]

"Here, here is the land we have been seeking."

All rushed to the bows. As the ship sailed on and they came nearer, they saw a lovely island. Mountains, towering peak on peak, with deep green valleys between brown rocky heights hung with vines, and the great ocean breakers booming in one white line of foaming surf on the reef of living coral, made it look like a vision of fairyland.

They had discovered Rarotonga.

But what of the people of the island?

They were said to be cannibals.

Would they receive the missionaries with clubs and spears? Who would go ashore?

On board the ship were brown South Sea men from the island where John Williams lived. They had burned their idols, and now they too were missionaries of Jesus Christ. Their leader was a fearless young man, Papeiha. He was so daring that once, when everybody else was afraid to go from the ship to a cannibal island, he bound his Bible in his loin cloth, tied them to the top of his head, and swam ashore, defying the sharks, and unafraid of the still more cruel islanders.

So at Rarotonga, when the call came, "Who will go ashore?" and a canoe was let down from the ship's side, two men, Papeiha and his friend Vahineino,[18] leapt into it. Those two fearlessly paddled towards the shore, which was now one brown stretch of Rarotongans crowded together to see this strange ship with wings that had sailed from over the sea's edge.

The Rarotongans seemed friendly; so Papeiha and Vahineino, who knew the ways of the water from babyhood and could swim before they could walk, waited for a great Pacific breaker, and then swept in on her foaming crest. The canoe grated on the shore. They walked up the beach under the shade of a grove of trees and said to the Rarotongan king, Makea,[19] and his people:

"We have come to tell you that many of the islands of the sea have burned their idols. Once we in those islands pierced each other with spears and beat each other to death with clubs; we brutally treated our women, and the children taken in war were strung together by their ears like fish on a line. To-day we come--before you have destroyed each other altogether in your wars--to tell you of the great God, our Father, who through His Son Jesus Christ has taught us how to live as brothers."

King Makea said he was pleased to hear these things, and came in his canoe to the ship to take the other native teachers on shore with him. The ship stood off for the night, for the ocean there is too deep for anchorage.

Papeiha and his brown friends, with their wives, went ashore. Night fell, and they were preparing to sleep, when, above the thud and hiss of the waves they heard the noise of approaching crowds. The footsteps and the talking came nearer, while the little group of Christians listened intently. At last a chief, carried by his warriors, came near. He was the fiercest and most powerful chief on the island.

When he came close to Papeiha and his friends, the chief demanded that the wife of one of the Christian teachers should be given to him, so that he might take her away with him as his twentieth wife. The teachers argued with the chief, the woman wept; but he ordered the woman to be seized and taken off. She resisted, as did the others. Their clothes were torn to tatters by the ferocious Rarotongans. All would have been over with the Christians, had not Tapairu,[20] a brave Rarotongan woman and the cousin of the king, opposed the chiefs and even fought with her hands to save the teacher's wife. At last the fierce chief gave in, and Papeiha and his friends, before the sun had risen, hurried to the beach, leapt into their canoe and paddled swiftly to the ship.

"We must wait and come to this island another day when the people are more friendly," said every one--except Papeiha, who never would turn back. "Let me stay with them," said he.

He knew that he might be slain and eaten by the savage cannibals on the island. But without fuss, leaving everything he had upon the ship except his clothes and his native Testament, he dropped into his canoe, seized the paddle, and with swift, strong strokes that never faltered, drove the canoe skimming over the rolling waves till it leapt to the summit of a breaking wave and ground upon the shore.

The savages came jostling and waving spears and clubs as they crowded round him.

"Let us take him to Makea."

So Papeiha was led to the chief. As he walked he heard them shouting to one another, "I'll have his hat," "I'll have his jacket," "I'll have his shirt."

At length he reached the chief, who looked and said, "Speak to us, O man, that we may know why you persist in coming."

"I come," he answered, looking round on all the people, "so that you may all learn of the true God, and that you, like all the people in the far-off islands of the sea, may take your gods made of wood, of birds' feathers and of cloth, and burn them."

A roar of anger and horror burst from the people. "What!" they cried, "burn the gods! What gods shall we then have? What shall we do without the gods?"

They were angry, but there was something in the bold face of Papeiha that kept them from slaying him. They allowed him to stay, and did not kill him.

Soon after this, Papeiha one day heard shrieking and shouting and wild roars as of men in a frenzy. He saw crowds of people round the gods offering food to them; the priests with faces blackened with charcoal and with bodies painted with stripes of red and yellow, the warriors with great waving head-dresses of birds' feathers and white sea-shells. Papeiha, without taking any thought of the peril that he rushed into, went into the midst of the people and said:

"Why do you act so foolishly? Why do you take a log of wood and carve it, and then offer it food? It is only fit to be burned. Some day soon you shall make these very gods fuel for fire." So with the companion who came to help him, brown Papeiha went in and out of the island just as brave Paul went in and out in the island of Cyprus and Wilfrid in Britain. He would take his stand, now under a grove of bananas on a great stone, and now in a village, where the people from the huts gathered round, and again on the beach, where he would lift up his voice above the boom of the ocean breakers to tell the story of Jesus. And some of those degraded savages became Christians.

One day he was surprised to see one of the priests come to him leading his ten-year-old boy.

"Take care of my boy," said the priest. "I am going to burn my god, and I do not want my god's anger to hurt the boy. Ask your God to protect him." So the priest went home.

Next morning quite early, before the heat of the sun was great, Papeiha looked out and saw the priest tottering along with bent and aching shoulders. On his back was his cumbrous wooden god. Behind the priest came a furious crowd, waving their arms and crying out:

"Madman, madman, the god will kill you."

"You may shout," answered the priest, "but you will not change me. I am going to worship Jehovah, the God of Papeiha." And with that he threw down the god at the feet of the teachers. One of them ran and brought a saw, and first cut off its head and then sawed it into logs. Some of the Rarotongans rushed away in dread. Others--even some of the newly converted Christians--hid in the bush and peered through the leaves to see what would happen. Papeiha lit a fire; the logs were thrown on; the first Rarotongan idol was burned.

"You will die," cried the priests of the fallen god. But to show that the god was just a log of wood, the teachers took a bunch of bananas, placed them on the ashes where the fire had died down, and roasted them. Then they sat down and ate the bananas.

The watching, awe-struck people looked to see the teachers fall dead, but nothing happened. The islanders then began to wonder whether, after all, the God of Papeiha was not the true God. Within a year they had got together hundreds of their wooden idols, and had burned them in enormous bonfires which flamed on the beach and lighted up the dark background of trees. Those bonfires could be seen far out across the Pacific Ocean, like a beacon light.

To-day the flames of love which Papeiha bravely lighted, through perils by water and club and cannibal feast, have shone right across the ocean, and some of the grandchildren of those very Rarotongans who were cannibals when Papeiha went there, have sailed away, as we shall see later on, to preach Papeiha's gospel of the love of God to the far-off cannibal Papuans on the steaming shores of New Guinea.

FOOTNOTES:

[Footnote 16: P[)a]-pay-ee-h[)a].]

[Footnote 17: Tay-ee-ay: ta-oo-a: fay-noo-[)a]: nay-ee.]

[Footnote 18: Va-hee-nay-ee-n[=o].]

[Footnote 19: M[)a]-kay-[)a].]

[Footnote 20: T[)a]-p[=a]-ee-roo.]

CHAPTER VII

THE DAYBREAK CALL

John Williams (Date of Incident, 1839)

Two men leaned on the rail of the brig Camden as she swept slowly along the southern side of the Island of Erromanga in the Western Pacific. A steady breeze filled her sails. The sea heaved in long, silky billows. The red glow of the rising sun was changing to the full, clear light of morning.

The men, as they talked, scanned the coast-line closely. There was the grey, stone-covered beach, and, behind the beach, the dense bush and the waving fronds of palms. Behind the palms rose the volcanic hills of the island. The elder man straightened himself and looked keenly to the bay from which a canoe was swiftly gliding.

He was a broad, sturdy man, with thick brown hair over keen watchful eyes. His open look was fearless and winning. His hands, which grasped the rail, had both the strength and the skill of the trained mechanic and the writer. For John Williams could build a ship, make a boat and sail them both against any man in all the Pacific. He could work with his hammer at the forge in the morning, make a table at his joiner's bench in the afternoon, preach a powerful sermon in the evening, and write a chapter of the most thrilling of books on missionary travel through the night. Yet next morning would see him in his ship, with her sails spread, moving out into the open Pacific, bound for a distant island.

"It is strange," Williams was saying to his friend Mr. Cunningham, "but I have not slept all through the night."

How came it that this man, who for over twenty years had faced tempests by sea, who had never flinched before perils from savage men and from fever, on the shores of a hundred islands in the South Seas, should stay awake all night as his ship skirted the strange island of Erromanga?

It was because, having lived for all those years among the coral islands of the brown Polynesians of the Eastern Pacific, he was now sailing to the New

Hebrides, where the fierce black cannibal islanders of the Western Pacific slew one another. As he thought of the fierce men of Erromanga he thought of the waving forests of brown hands he had seen, the shouts of "Come back again to us!" that he had heard as he left his own islands. He knew how those people loved him in the Samoan Islands, but he could not rest while others lay far off who had never heard the story of Jesus. "I cannot be content," he said, "within the narrow limits of a single reef."

But the black islanders were wild men who covered their dark faces with soot and painted their lips with flaming red, yet their cruel hearts were blacker than their faces, and their anger more fiery than their scarlet lips. They were treacherous and violent savages who would smash a skull by one blow with a great club; or leaping on a man from behind, would cut through his spine with a single stroke of their tomahawks, and then drag him off to their cannibal oven.

John Williams cared so much for his work of telling the islanders about God their Father, that he lay awake wondering how he could carry it on among these wild people. It never crossed his mind that he should hold back to save himself from danger. It was for this work that he had crossed the world.

"Let down the whale-boat." His voice rang out without a tremor of fear. His eyes were on the canoe in which three black Erromangans were paddling across the bay. As the boat touched the water, he and the crew of four dropped into her, with Captain Morgan and two friends, Harris and Cunningham. The oars dipped and flashed in the morning sun as the whale-boat flew along towards the canoe. When they reached it, Williams spoke in the dialects of his other islands, but none could the three savages in the canoe understand. So he gave them some beads and fish-hooks as a present to show that he was a friend and again his boat shot away toward the beach.

They pulled to a creek where a brook ran down in a lovely valley between two mountains. On the beach stood some Erromangan natives, with their eyes (half fierce, half frightened) looking out under their matted jungle of hair.

Picking up a bucket from the boat, Williams held it out to the chief and made signs to show that he wished for water from the brook. The chief took the bucket, and, turning, ran up the beach and disappeared. For a quarter of an hour they waited; and for half an hour. At last, when the sun was now high in the sky, the chief returned with the water.

Williams drank from the water to show his friendliness. Then his friend, Harris, swinging himself over the side of the boat, waded ashore through the cool, sparkling, shallow water and sat down. The natives ran away, but soon came back with cocoa-nuts and opened them for him to drink.

* * * * *

"See," said Williams, "there are boys playing on the beach; that is a good sign."

"Yes," answered Captain Morgan, "but there are no women, and when the savages mean mischief they send their women away."

Williams now waded ashore and Cunningham followed him. Captain Morgan stopped to throw out the anchor of his little boat and then stepped out and went ashore, leaving his crew of four brown islanders resting on their oars.

Williams and his two companions scrambled up the stony beach over the grey stones and boulders alongside the tumbling brook for over a hundred yards. Turning to the right they were lost to sight from the water-edge. Captain Morgan was just following them when he heard a terrified yell from the crew in the boat.

Williams and his friends had gone into the bush, Harris in front, Cunningham next, and Williams last. Suddenly Harris, who had disappeared in the bush, rushed out followed by yelling savages with clubs. Harris rushed down the bank of the brook, stumbled, and fell in. The water dashed over him, and the Erromangans, with the red fury of slaughter in their eyes, leapt in and beat in his skull with clubs.

Cunningham, with a native at his heels with lifted club, stooped, picked up a great pebble and hurled it full at the savage who was pursuing him. The man was stunned. Turning again, Cunningham leapt safely into the boat.

Williams, leaving the brook, had rushed down the beach to leap into the sea.

Reaching the edge of the water, where the beach falls steeply into the sea, he slipped on a pebble and fell into the water.

Cunningham, from the boat, hurled stones at the natives rushing at Williams, who lay prostrate in the water with a savage over him with uplifted club. The club fell, and other Erromangans, rushing in, beat him with their clubs and shot their arrows into him until the ripples of the beach ran red with his blood.

The hero who had carried the flaming torch of peace on earth to the savages on scores of islands across the great Pacific Ocean was dead--the first martyr of Erromanga.

* * * * *

When The Camden sailed back to Samoa, scores of canoes put out to meet her. A brown Samoan guided the first canoe.

"Missi William," he shouted.

"He is dead," came the answer.

The man stood as though stunned. He dropped his paddle; he drooped his head, and great tears welled out from the eyes of this dark islander and ran down his cheeks.

The news spread like wildfire over the islands, and from all directions came the natives crying in multitudes:

"Aue,[21] Williamu, Aue, Tama!" (Alas, Williams, Alas, our Father!)

And the chief Malietoa,[22] coming into the presence of Mrs. Williams, cried:

"Alas, Williamu, Williamu, our father, our father! He has turned his face from us! We shall never see him more! He that brought us the good word of Salvation is gone! O cruel heathen, they know not what they did! How great a man they have destroyed!"

John Williams, the torch-bearer of the Pacific, whom the brown men loved, the great pioneer, who dared death on the grey beach of Erromanga, sounds a morning bugle-call to us, a Reveill?to our slumbering camps:

"The daybreak call, Hark how loud and clear I hear it sound; Swift to your places, swift to the head of the army, Pioneers, O Pioneers!"[23]

FOOTNOTES:

[Footnote 21: A-oo-ay.]

[Footnote 22: M[)a]-lee-ay-to-[)a].]

[Footnote 23: Walt Whitman.]

CHAPTER VIII

KAPIOLANI, THE HEROINE OF HAWAII

Kapiolani (Date of Incident, 1824)

"PAN 閇 24] the all-terrible, the fire goddess, will hurl her thunder and her stones, and will slay you," cried the angry priests of Hawaii.[25] "You no longer pay your sacrifices to her. Once you gave her hundreds of hogs, but now you give nothing. You worship the new God Jehovah. She, the great PAN will come upon you, she and the Husband of Thunder, with the Fire-Thruster, and the Red-Fire Cloud-Queen, they will destroy you altogether."

The listening Hawaiians shuddered as they saw the shaggy priests calling down the anger of PAN One of the priests was a gigantic man over six feet five inches high, whose strength was so terrible that he could leap at his victims and break their bones by his embrace.

Away there in the volcanic island[26] in the centre of the greatest ocean in the world--the Pacific Ocean--they had always as children been taught to fear the great goddess.

They were Christians; but they had only been Christians for a short time, and they still trembled at the name of the goddess PAN who lived up in the mountains in the boiling crater of the fiery volcano, and ruled their island.

Their fathers had told them how she would get angry, and would pour out red-hot rivers of molten stone that would eat up all the trees and people and run hissing into the Pacific Ocean. There to that day was that river of stone--a long tongue of cold, hard lava--stretching down to the shore of the island, and here across the trees on the mountain-top could be seen, even now, the smoke of her anger. Perhaps, after all, PANwas greater than Jehovah--she was certainly terrible--and she was very near!

"If you do not offer fire to her, as you used to do," the priests went on, "she will pour down her fire into the sea and kill all your fish. She will fill up your fishing grounds with the pahoehoe[27] (lava), and you will starve. Great is PANand greatly to be feared."

The priests were angry because the preaching of the missionaries had led many away from the worship of PANwhich, of course, meant fewer hogs for themselves; and now the whole nation on Hawaii, that volcanic island of the seas, seemed to be deserting her.

The people began to waver under the threats, but a brown-faced woman, with strong, fearless eyes that looked out with scorn on PANpriests, was not to be terrified.

"It is Kapiolani,[28] the chieftainess," murmured the people to one another. "She is Christian; will she forsake Jehovah and return to PAN"

Only four years before this, Kapiolani had--according to the custom of the Hawaiian chieftainesses, married many husbands, and she had given way to drinking habits. Then she had become a Christian, giving up her drinking and sending away all her husbands save one. She had thrown away her idols and now taught the people in their huts the story of Christ.

"PANis nought," she declared, "I will go to Kilawea,[29] the mountain of the fires where the smoke and stones go up, and PANshall not touch me. My God, Jehovah, made the mountain and the fires within it too, as He made us all."

So it was noised through the island that Kapiolani, the queenly, would defy PANthe goddess. The priests threatened her with awful torments of fire from the goddess; her people pleaded with her not to dare the fires of Kilawea. But Kapiolani pressed on, and eighty of her people made up their minds to go with her. She climbed the mountain paths, through lovely valleys hung with trees, up and up to where the hard rocky lava-river cut the feet of those who walked upon it.

Day by day they asked her to go back, and always she answered, "If I am destroyed you may believe in PAN if I live you must all believe in the true God, Jehovah."

As she drew nearer to the crater she saw the great cloud of smoke that came up from the volcano and felt the heat of its awful fires. But she did not draw back.

As she climbed upward she saw by the side of the path low bushes, and on them beautiful red and yellow berries, growing in clusters. The berries were like large currants.

"It is chelo,"[30] said the priests, "it is PANs berry. You must not touch them unless we ask her. She will breathe fire on you."

Kapiolani broke off a branch from one of the bushes regardless of the horrified faces of the priests. And she ate the berries, without stopping to ask the goddess for her permission.

She carried a branch of the berries in her hand. If she had told them what she was going to do they would have been frenzied with fear and horror.

Up she climbed until the full terrors of the boiling crater of Kilawea burst on her sight. Before her an immense gulf yawned in the shape of the crescent moon, eight miles in circumference and over a thousand feet deep. Down in the smoking hollow, hundreds of feet beneath her, a lake of fiery lava rolled in flaming waves against precipices of rock. This ever-moving lake of molten fire is called: "The House of Everlasting Burning." This surging lake was dotted with tiny mountain islets, and, from the tops of their little peaks, pyramids of flame blazed and columns of grey smoke went up. From some of these little islands streams of blazing lava rolled down into the lake of fire. The air was filled with the roar of the furnaces of flame.

Even the fearless Kapiolani stood in awe as she looked. But she did not flinch, though here and there, as she walked, the crust of the lava cracked under her feet and the ground was hot with hidden fire.

She came to the very edge of the crater. To come so far without offering hogs and fish to the fiery goddess was in itself enough to bring a fiery river of molten lava upon her. Kapiolani offered nothing save defiance. Audacity, they thought, could go no further.

Here, a priestess of PANcame, and raising her hands in threat denounced death on the head of Kapiolani if she came further. Kapiolani pulled from her robe a book. In it--for it was her New Testament--she read to the priestess of the one true, loving Father-God.

Then Kapiolani did a thing at which the very limbs of those who watched trembled and shivered. She went to the edge of the crater and stepped over onto a jutting rock and let herself down and down toward the sulphurous burning lake. The ground cracked under her feet and sulphurous steam hissed through crevices in the rock, as though the demons of PANfumed in their frenzy. Hundreds of staring, wondering eyes followed her, fascinated and yet horrified.

Then she stood on a ledge of rock, and, offering up prayer and praise to the God of all, Who made the volcano and Who made her, she cast the PANberries into the lake, and sent stone after stone down into the flaming lava. It was the most awful insult that could be offered to PAN Now surely she would leap up in fiery anger, and, with a hail of burning stones, consume Kapiolani. But nothing happened; and Kapiolani, turning, climbed the steep ascent of the crater edge and at last stood again unharmed among her people. She spoke to her people, telling them again that Jehovah made the fires. She called on them all to sing to His praise and, for the first time, there rang across the crater of Kilawea the song of Christians. The power of the priests was gone, and from that hour the people all over that island who had trembled and hesitated between PANand Christ turned to the worship of our Lord Jesus, the Son of God the Father Almighty.

FOOTNOTES:

[Footnote 24: Pay-lay.]

[Footnote 25: Hah-wye-ee.]

[Footnote 26: Discovered by Captain Cook in 1778. The first Christian missionaries landed in 1819. Now the island is ruled by the United States of America.]

[Footnote 27: Pa-h[=o]-?h[=o]-?]

[Footnote 28: Kah-p-[=o]-l[)a]-n. She was high female chief, in her own right, of a large district.]

[Footnote 29: Kil-a-wee-[)a]. The greatest active volcano in the world.]

[Footnote 30: Chay-lo.]

CHAPTER IX

THE CANOE OF ADVENTURE

Elikana (Date of Incident, 1861)

"I know not where His islands lift Their fronded palms in air; I only know I cannot drift Beyond His love and care."

I

Manihiki Island looked like a tiny anchored canoe far away across the Pacific, as Elikana glanced back from his place at the tiller. He sang, meantime, quietly to himself an air that still rang in his ears, the tune that he and his brother islanders had sung in praise of the Power and Providence of God at the services on Manihiki. For the Christian people of the Penrhyn group of South Sea Islands had come together in April, 1861, for their yearly meeting, paddling from the different quarters in their canoes through the white surge of the breakers that thunder day and night round the island.

Elikana looked ahead to where his own island of Rakahanga grew clearer every moment on the sky-line ahead of them, though each time his craft dropped into the trough of the sea between the green curves of the league-long ocean rollers the island was lost from sight.

He and his six companions were sailing back over the thirty miles between Manihiki and Rakahanga, two of the many little lonely ocean islands that stud the Pacific like stars.

They sailed a strange craft, for it cannot be called raft or canoe or hut. It was all these and yet was neither. Two canoes, forty-eight feet long, sailed side by side. Between the canoes were spars, stretching across from one to the other, lashed to each boat and making a platform between them six feet wide. On this was built a hut, roofed with the beautiful braided leaves of the cocoa-nut palm.

Overhead stretched the infinite sky. Underneath lay thousands of fathoms of blue-green ocean, whose cold, hidden deeps among the mountains and valleys of the awful ocean under-world held strange goblin fish-shapes. And on the surface this hut of leaves and bamboo swung dizzily between sky and ocean on the frail canoes. And in the canoes and the hut were six brown Rakahangan men, two women, and a chubby, dark-eyed child, who sat contented and tired, being lapped to sleep by the swaying waters.

Above them the great sail made of matting of fibre, strained in the breeze that drove them nearer to the haven where they would be. Already they could see the gleam of the Rakahanga beach with the rim of silver where the waves broke into foam. Then the breeze dropped. The fibre-sail flapped uneasily against the mast, while the two little canvas sails hung loosely, as the wind, with little warning, swung round, and smiting them in the face began to drive them back into the ocean again.

Elikana and his friends knew the sea almost like fish, from the time they were babies. And they were little troubled by the turn of the breeze, save that it would delay their homecoming. They tried in vain to make headway. Slowly, but surely they were driven back from land, till they could see that there was no other thing but just to turn about and let her run back to Manihiki. In the canoes were enough cocoa-nuts to feed them for days if need be, and two large calabashes of water.

The swift night fell, but the wind held strong, and one man sat at the tiller while two others baled out the water that leaked into the canoes. They kept a keen watch, expecting to sight Manihiki; but when the dawn flashed out of the sky in the East, where the island should have been, there was neither Manihiki nor any other land at all. They had no chart nor compass; north and south and east and west stretched the wastes of the Pacific for hundreds of leagues. Only here and there in the ocean, and all unseen to them, like little groups of mushrooms on a limitless prairie, lay groups of islets.

They might, indeed, sail for a year without ever sighting any land; and one storm-driven wave of the great ocean could smite their little egg-shell craft to the bottom of the sea.

They gathered together in the hut and with anxious faces talked of what they might do. They knew that far off to the southwest lay the islands of Samoa, and Rarotonga. So they set the bows of their craft southward. Morning grew to blazing noon and fell to evening and night, and nothing did they see save the glittering sparkling waters of the uncharted ocean, cut here and there by the cruel fin of a waiting shark. It was Saturday when they started; and night fell seven times while their wonderful hut-boat crept southward along the water, till the following Friday. Then the wind changed, and, springing up from the south, drove them wearily back once more in their tracks, and then bore them eastward.

For another week they drove before the breeze, feeding on the cocoa-nuts. But the water in the calabashes was gone. Then on the morning of the second Friday, the fourteenth day of their sea-wanderings, just when the sun in mid heaven was blazing its noon-heat upon them and most of the little crew were lying under the shade of the hut and the sail to doze away the hours of tedious hunger, they heard the cry of "Land!" and leaping to their feet gazed ahead at the welcome sight. With sail and paddle they urged the craft on toward the island.

Then night fell, and with it squalls of wind and rain came and buffeted them till they had to forsake the paddles for the bailing-vessels to keep the boat afloat. Taking down the sails they spread them flat to catch the pouring rain, and then poured this precious fresh water--true water of life to them--into their calabashes. But when morning came no land could be seen anywhere. It was as though the island had been a land of enchantment and mirage, and now had faded away. Yet hope sprang in them erect and glad next day when land was sighted again; but the sea and the wind, as though driven by the spirits of contrariness, smote them back.

For two more days they guided the canoe with the tiller and tried to set her in one steady direction. Then, tired and out of heart, after sixteen days of ceaseless and useless effort, they gave it up and let her drift, for the winds and currents to take her where they would.

At night each man stood in his canoe almost starving and parched with thirst, with aching back, stooping to dip the water from the canoe and rising to pour it over the side. For hour after hour, while the calm moon slowly climbed the sky, each slaved at his dull task. Lulled by the heave and fall of the long-backed rollers as they slid under the keels of the canoes, the men nearly dropped asleep where they stood. The quiet waters crooned to them like a mother singing an old lullaby--crooned and called, till a voice deep within them said, "It is better to lie down and sleep and die than to live and fight and starve."

Then a moan from the sleeping child, or a sight of a streaming ray of moonlight on the face of its mother would send that nameless Voice shivering back to its deep hiding-place--and the man would stoop and bail again.

Each evening as it fell saw their anxious eyes looking west and north and south for land, and always there was only the weary waste of waters. And as the sun rose, they hardly dared open their eyes to the unbroken rim of blue-grey that circled them like a steel prison. They saw the thin edge of the moon grow to full blaze and then fade to a corn sickle again as days and nights grew to weeks and a whole month had passed.

Every morning, as the pearl-grey sea turned to pink and then to gleaming blue, they knelt on the raft between the canoes and turned their faces up to their Father in prayer, and never did the sun sink behind the rim of waters without the sound of their voices rising into the limitless sky with thanks for safe-keeping.

Slowly the pile of cocoa-nuts lessened. Each one of them with its sweet milk and flesh was more precious to them than a golden chalice set with rubies. The drops of milk that dripped from them were more than ropes of pearls.

At last eight Sundays had followed one upon another; and now at the end of the day there was only the half of one cocoa-nut remaining. When that was gone--all would be over. So they knelt down under the cloudless sky on an evening calm and beautiful. They were on that invisible line in the Great Pacific where the day ends and begins. Those seven on the tiny craft were, indeed, we cannot but believe, the last worshippers in all the great world-house of God as Sunday drew to its end just where they were. Was it to be the last time that they would pray to God in this life?

Prayer ended; night was falling. Elikana the leader, who had kept their spirits from utterly failing, stood up and gazed out with great anxious eyes before the last light should fail.

"Look, there upon the edge of the sea where the sun sets. Is it--" He could hardly dare to believe that it was not the mirage of his weary brain. But one and another and then all peered out through the swiftly waning light and saw that indeed it was land.

Then a squall of wind sprang up, blowing them away from the land. Was this last hope, by a fine ecstasy of torture, to be dangled before them and then snatched away? But with the danger came the help; with the wind came the rain; cool, sweet, refreshing, life-giving water. Then the squall of wind dropped and changed. They hoisted the one sail that had not blown to tatters, and drove for land.

Yet their most awful danger still lay before them. The roar of the breakers on the cruel coral reef caught their ears. But there was nothing for it but to risk the peril. They were among the breakers which caught and tossed them on like eggshells. The scourge of the surf swept them; a woman, a man--even the child, were torn from them and ground on the ghastly teeth of the coral. Five were swept over with the craft into the still, blue lagoon, and landing they fell prone upon the shore, just breathing and no more, after the giant buffeting of the thundering rollers, following the long, slow starvation of their wonderful journey in the hut on the canoes among "the waters of the wondrous isles."

"Wake: the silver dusk returning Up the beach of darkness brims, And the ship of sunrise burning Strands upon the eastern rims."

II

Thrown up by the ocean in the darkness like driftwood, Elikana and his companions lay on the grey shore. Against the dim light of the stars and beyond the beach of darkness they could see the fronds of the palms waving. The five survivors were starving, and the green cocoa-nuts hung above them, filled with food and drink. But their bodies, broken and tormented as they were by hunger and the battering breakers, refused even to rise and climb for the food that meant life. So they lay there, as though dead.

* * * * *

Over the ridge of the beach came a man. His pale copper skin shone in the fresh sunlight of the morning. His quick black eyes were caught by the sight of torn clothing hanging on a bush. Moving swiftly down the beach of pounded coral, he saw a man lying with arms thrown out, face downward. Turning the body over Faivaatala[31] found that the man was dead. Taking the body in his arms he staggered with it up the beach, and placed it under the shade of the trees. Returning he found the living five. Their gaunt bodies and the broken craft on the shore told him without words the story of their long drifting over the wilderness of the waters.

Without stopping to waste words in empty sympathy with starving men, Faivaatala ran to the nearest cocoa-nut tree and, climbing it, threw down luscious nuts. Those below quickly knocked off the tops, drank deep draughts of the cool milk and then ate. Coming down again, Faivaatala kindled a fire and soon had some fish grilling for these strange wanderers thrown up on the tiny islet.

They had no time to thank him before he ran off and swiftly paddled to

Motutala, the island where he lived, to tell the story of these strange castaways. He came back with other helpers in canoes, and the five getting aboard were swiftly paddled to Motutala.

As the canoes skimmed over the surface of the great lagoon Elikana and his friends could see, spread out in a great semi-circle that stretched to the horizon, the long low coral islets crowned with palms which form part of the Ellice Islands.

The islanders, men, women, and children, ran down the beach to see the newcomers and soon had set apart huts for them and made them welcome. Elikana gathered them round him, and began to tell them about the love of Jesus and the protecting care of God the Father. It all seemed strange to them, but quickly they learned from him, and he began to teach them and their children. This went on for four months, till one day Elikana said: "I must go away and learn more so that I can teach you more."

But they had become so fond of Elikana that they said: "No, you must not leave us," and it was only when he promised to come back with another teacher to help him, that they could bring themselves to part with him. So when a ship came to the island to trade in cocoa-nuts Elikana went aboard and sailed to Samoa to the London Missionary Society's training college there at Malua.

* * * * *

"A ship! A ship!" The cry was taken up through the island, and the people running down the beach saw a large sailing vessel. Boats put down and sculls flashed as sailors pulled swiftly to the shore.

They landed and the people gathered round to see and to hear what they would say.

"Come onto our ship," said these men, who had sailed there from Peru, "and we will show you how you can be rich with many knives and much calico."

But the islanders shook their heads and said they would stay where they were. Then a wicked white man named Tom Rose, who lived on the island

and knew how much the people were looking forward to the day when Elikana would come back to teach them, went to the traders and whispered what he knew to them.

So the Peruvian traders, with craft shining in their eyes, turned again to the islanders and said: "If you will come with us, we will take you where you will be taught all that men can know about God."

At this the islanders broke out into glad cries and speaking to one another said: "Let us go and learn these things."

The day came for sailing, and as the sun rose, hundreds of brown feet were running to the beach, children dancing with excitement, women saying "Goodbye" to their husbands--men, who for the first time in all their lives were to leave their tiny islet for the wonderful world beyond the ocean.

So two hundred of them went on board. The sails were hoisted and they went away never to return; sailed away not to learn of Jesus, but to the sting of the lash and the shattering bullet, the bondage of the plantations, and to death at the hands of those merciless beasts of prey, the Peruvian slavers.

* * * * *

Years passed and a little fifty-ton trading vessel came to anchor outside the reef. One man and then another and another got down into the little boat and pulled for the shore. Elikana had returned. The women and children ran down to meet him--but few men were there, for nearly all had gone.

"Where is this one? Where is the other?" cried Elikana, with sad face as he looked around on them.

"Gone, gone," came the answer; "carried away by the man-stealing ships."

Elikana turned to the white missionary who had come with him, to ask what they could do.

"We will leave Joane and his wife here," replied Mr. Murray.

* * * * *

So a teacher from Samoa stayed there and taught the people, while Elikana went to begin work in an island near by.

To-day a white lady missionary has gone to live in the Ellice Islands, and the people are Christians, and no slave-trader can come to snatch them away.

So there sailed over the waters of the wondrous isles first the boat of sunrise and then the ship of darkness, and last of all the ship of the Peace of God. The ship of darkness had seemed for a time to conquer, but her day is now over; and to-day on that beach, as the sunlight brims over the edge of the sea, and a new Lord's Day dawns, you may hear the islanders sing their praise to the Light of the World, Who shines upon them and keeps them safe.

FOOTNOTES:

[Footnote 31: F[)a]-ee-v[)a] t[)a] l[=a].]

CHAPTER X

THE ARROWS OF SANTA CRUZ

Bishop Patteson (Date of Incident--August 15th, 1864)

The brown crew of The Southern Cross breathed freely again as the anchor swung into place and the schooner began to nose her way out into the open Pacific. They were hardened to dangers, but the Island of Tawny Cannibals had strained their nerve, by its hourly perils from club and flying arrow. The men were glad to see their ship's bows plunge freely again through the long-backed rollers.

As they set her course to the Island of Santa Cruz the crew talked together of the men of the island they had left. In his cabin sat a great bronzed bearded man writing a letter to his own people far away on the other side of the world. Here are the very words that he wrote as he told the story of one of the dangers through which they had just passed on the island:

"As I sat on the beach with a crowd about me, most of them suddenly jumped up and ran off. Turning my head I saw a man (from the boat they saw two) coming to me with club uplifted. I remained sitting and held out a few fish-hooks to him, but one or two men jumped up and, seizing him by the waist, forced him off.

"After a few minutes I went back to the boat. I found out that a poor fellow called Moliteum was shot dead two months ago by a white trader for stealing a bit of calico. The wonder was, not that they wanted to avenge the death of their kinsman, but that others should have prevented it. How could they possibly know that I was not one of the wicked set? Yet they did.... The plan of going among the people unarmed makes them regard me as a friend."

Then he says of these men who had just tried to kill him: "The people, though constantly fighting, and cannibals and the rest of it, are to me very attractive."

The ship sailed on till they heard ahead of them the beating of the surf on the reef of Santa Cruz. Behind the silver line of the breakers the waving fronds of her palms came into sight. They put The Southern Cross in, cast anchor, and let a boat down from her side. Into the boat tumbled a British sailor named Pearce, a young twenty-year-old Englishman named Atkin, and three brown South-Sea Island boys from the missionary training college for native teachers on Norfolk Island, and their leader, Bishop Patteson, the white man who, having faced the clubs of savages on a score of islands, never flinched from walking into peril again to lead them to know of "the best Man in the world, Jesus Christ." These brown boys were young helpers of Bishop Patteson. And one of them especially, Fisher Young, would have died for his great white leader gladly. They were like father and son.

The reef, covered at mid-tide with curling waters mottled with the foam of the broken waves, was alive with men; while the beach beyond was black with crowds of the wild islanders who had come down to see the strange visitors from the ship. The four men sculled the boat on to the edge of the reef and then rested on their oars as Patteson swung himself over the side into the cool water. He waded across the reef between the hosts of savages, and in every hand was a club or spear or a six-foot wooden bow with an arrow ready to notch in its bamboo string.

Patteson had come to make friends with them. So he entered a dark wattled house and sat down to talk. The doorway was filled with the faces of wondering men. As he looked on them a strange gleam of longing came into his eyes and a smile of great tenderness softened the strength of his brown face--the longing and the tenderness of a shepherd looking for wandering sheep who are lost on the wild mountains of the world.

Then he rose, left the house, and went back to the boat. The water was now one seething cauldron of men--walking, splashing, swimming. Some, as Patteson climbed into his boat, caught hold of the gunwale and could hardly be made to loosen their hold. The four young fellows in the boat swung their oars and got her under way, but they had made barely half a dozen strokes when, without warning, an arrow whizzed through the air into the boat. A cloud of arrows followed.

Six canoes were now filled with savage Santa Cruzans, who surrounded the boat and joined in the shooting. Patteson, who was in the stern between his boys and the bowmen, had not shipped the rudder, so he held it up, as the boat shot ahead of the canoes, to shield off arrows.

Turning round to see whither his now rudderless boat was being pulled, he saw that they were heading for a little bay in the reef, which would have wrecked their hopes of safety.

"Pull, port oars, pull on steadily," shouted Patteson; and they made for The Southern Cross.

As he called to them he saw Pearce, the young British sailor, lying between the thwarts with the long shaft of an arrow in his chest, and a young Norfolk Islander with an arrow under his left eye. The arrows flew around them in clouds, and suddenly Fisher Young--the nineteen-year-old Polynesian whom he loved as a son--who was pulling stroke, gave a faint scream. He was shot through the left wrist.

"Look out, sir! close to you," cried one of his crew. But the arrows were all around him. All the way to the schooner the canoes skimmed over the water chasing the boat. The four youths, including the wounded, pulled on bravely and steadily. At last they reached the ship and climbed on board, while the canoes--fearing vengeance from the men on the schooner--turned and fled.

Once aboard, Bishop Patteson knelt by the side of Pearce, drew out the arrow which had run more than five inches deep into his chest, and bound up his wound. Turning to Fisher, he found that the arrow had gone through the wrist and had broken off in the wound. Taking hold of the point of the arrow where it stood out on the lower side of the wrist, Patteson pulled it through, though the agony of the boy was very great.

The arrows were wooden-headed and not poisoned. The wounds seemed to be healing, but a few days later Fisher said, "I can't make out what makes my jaws feel so stiff."

Fisher Young was the grandson of fierce, foul Pitcairn Island cannibals, and was himself a brave and pure Christian lad. He had faced death with his master many times on coral reefs, in savage villages, on wild seas and under the clubs of Pacific islanders. Now he was face to face with something more difficult than a swift and dangerous adventure--the slow, dying agony of lockjaw. He grew steadily worse in spite of everything that Patteson could do.

Near to the end he said faintly, "Kiss me; I am very glad I was doing my duty. Tell my father that I was in the path of duty, and he will be so glad. Poor Santa Cruz people!"

He spoke in that way of the people who had killed him. The young brown hero lies to-day, as he would have wished, in the port that was named after the Bishop whom he loved, and who was his hero, Port Patteson.

"I loved him," said Patteson, "as I think I never loved anyone else." Fisher's love to his Bishop had been that of a youth to the hero whom he worships, but Patteson had led that brown islander still further, for he had taught the boy to love the Hero of all heroes, Jesus Christ.

CHAPTER XI

FIVE KNOTS IN A PALM LEAF

The Death of Patteson (Date of Incident, September 20th, 1871)

The masts of the schooner The Southern Cross swung gently to and fro across the darkening sky as the long, calm rollers of the Pacific slipped past her hull. Her bows spread only a ripple of water as the slight breeze bore her slowly towards the island of Nukapu.[32]

On deck stood a group of men, their brown faces turned to a tall, bearded man. As the light of the setting sun gleamed on his bronze face, it kindled his brave eyes and showed the grave smile that played about the corners of his mouth. They all looked on him with that worship which strong men give to a hero, who can be both brave and kindly. But "he wist not that his face shone" for them.

Patteson read to these young men from a Book; and the words that he read were these: "And they stoned Stephen, calling upon God and saying, 'Lord Jesus, receive my spirit.' And he knelt down and cried, with a loud voice, 'Lord, lay not this sin to their charge'; and when he had said this, he fell asleep."

When he had spoken to them strongly on these words and said how it may come to any man who worships Jesus to suffer so, Bishop Patteson and all except the man on watch went to their sleep. The South Sea Island men and the young Englishman who were there remembered all their lives what Patteson had said that evening; partly because these men themselves had seen him brave such a death as Stephen's again and again, and, indeed, they had themselves stood in peril by his side face to face with threatening savages, but even more because of the adventure that came to them on the next day.

At dawn they sighted land, and by eleven o'clock they were so near that they could see, shimmering in the heat of the midsummer sun, the white beach of coral sand and the drooping palms that make all the island of Nukapu green.[33] Looking out under their hands to the island, the men aboard The Southern Cross could see four great canoes, with their sails set, hovering like hawks about the circling reef which lay between them and the island. On the reef the blue waves beat and broke into a gleaming line of cool white foam.

The slight breeze was hardly strong enough to help the ship to make the island. It was as though she knew the danger of that day and would not carry Patteson and his men into the perils that lay hidden behind the beauty of that island of Nukapu.

Patteson knew the danger. He knew that, but a little time before their visit, white men had come in a ship, had let down their boats and rowed to the men of the island, had pretended to make friends, and then, shooting some and capturing others, had sped back to the ship, carrying off the captives to work for them on the island of Fiji. The law of the savages of the islands was "Blood for blood." And to them all white men belonged to one tribe. The peril that lay before Patteson was that they might attack him in revenge for the foul crime of those white traders.

Just before noon the order was given to lower a boat from The Southern Cross. Patteson went down into it, and sat in the stern, while Mr. Atkin (his English helper), Stephen Taroniara, James Minipa, and John Nonono came with him to row. The boat swung toward the reef. Between the reef and the island lay two miles of the blue and glittering lagoon.

By the time the boat reached the reef six canoes full of warriors had come together there. The tide was not high enough to float the boat across the reef. The Nukapuan natives said they would haul the boat up on to the reef, but the Bishop did not think it wise to consent. Then two of the savages said to "Bisipi," as they called the Bishop:

"Will you come into our canoe?"

Without a moment's hesitation, knowing that confidence was the best way to win them, he stepped into the canoe. As he entered they gave him a basket with yams and other fruit in it.

As the tide was low, the Bishop and the savages were obliged to wade over the reef, dragging the canoe across to the deeper lagoon within. The boat's crew of The Southern Cross stopped in the outer sea, drifting on the tide with the other four Nukapu canoes. They watched the Bishop cross the lagoon in the canoe and land far off upon the beach. Then he went from their sight.

The brown men and the white man in the boat were trying to talk to the islanders in the remaining canoes outside the reef, when suddenly a savage jumped up in the nearest canoe, not ten yards from them, and called out in his native language:

"Have you anything like this?"

He drew his bow to his ear and shot a yard arrow. His companions in the other canoes leapt to their feet and sent showers of arrows whizzing at the men in the boat, shouting as they aimed:

"This for New Zealand man, this for Bernu man, this for Motu man."

Pulling away with all their speed, Patteson's men were soon out of range, but an arrow had nailed John Nonono's cap to his head. Stephen lay in the bottom of the boat with six arrows in his chest and shoulders. Mr. Atkin, the white man, had one in his left shoulder.

They reached the ship and were helped on board. The arrow head was drawn out from Mr. Atkin's shoulder, and was found to be made of a sharpened human bone. No sooner was the arrow head out than Mr. Atkin leapt back into the boat, insisting on going back to find Patteson. He alone knew how and where the reef could be crossed on the tide that was now rising.

So they got a boat's crew from the ship, put a beaker full of water and some food in the boat, and pulled toward the reef.

At half-past four the tide was high enough to carry them across, and they rowed over, looking through their glasses anxiously at the white shore which was lined with brown figures. A canoe rowed out towards them bringing another canoe in tow. As the boat went towards the island, one canoe cast off the other, and went back; the second canoe drifted towards them slowly on the still waters of the blue lagoon.

As it came nearer they saw that in the middle of it lay Something motionless, covered with matting. They pulled alongside, leaned over the canoe, and lifted into their boat--the body of Patteson. The empty canoe now drifted away.

A yell went up from the savages on the shore. The boat was pulled towards the ship and then the body lifted up and laid on the deck. It had been rolled in the native matting as a shroud, tied at the head and feet. They unrolled the mat, and there on the face of the dead Bishop was still that wonderful, patient and winning smile, as of one who at the moment when his head was beneath the uplifted club said, "Lord, lay not this sin to their charge," and had then fallen asleep.

There was a palm leaf fastened over his breast. In its long leaflets five knots were made. On the body, in the head, the side, and the legs were five wounds. And five men in Fiji were at work in the plantations--men captured from Nukapu by brutal white traders.

It was the vengeance of the savage--the call of "blood for blood"; and the death of Patteson lies surely upon the head of those white traders who carried death and captivity to the white coral shore of Nukapu.

FOOTNOTES:

[Footnote 32: Noo-k[)a]-poo.]

[Footnote 33: Midsummer day on the Equator, September 21.]

CHAPTER XII

THE BOY OF THE ADVENTUROUS HEART

Chalmers, the Boy

(Born 1841, martyred 1901)

The rain had poured down in such torrents that even the hardy boys of Inverary in Scotland had been driven indoors. Now the sky had cleared, and the sun was shining again after the great storm. The boys were out again, and a group of them were walking toward the little stream of Aray which tumbled through the glen down to Loch Fyne. But the stream was "little" no longer.

As the boys came near to the place called "The Three Bridges," where a rough wooden bridge crossed the torrent, they walked faster towards the stream, for they could hear it roaring in a perfect flood which shook the timbers of the bridge. The great rainfall was running from the hills through a thousand streamlets into the main torrent.

Suddenly there came a shout and a scream. A boy dashed toward them saying that one of his schoolmates had fallen into the rushing water, and that the full spate of the Aray was carrying him away down to the sea. The boys stood horrified--all except one, who rushed forward, pulling off his jacket as he ran, leapt down the bank to the lower side of the bridge, and, clinging to the timber, held to it with one arm while he stretched out the other as the drowning boy was being carried under the bridge, seized him, and held him tightly with his left hand.

James Chalmers--the boy who had gone to the rescue--though only ten years old, could swim. Letting go of the bridge, while still holding the other boy with one arm, he allowed the current to carry them both down to where the branches hung over the bank to the water's surface. Seizing one of these, he dragged himself and the boy toward the bank, whence he was helped to dry land by his friends.

The boy whom young James Chalmers had saved belonged to a rival school. Often the wild-blooded boys (like their fierce Highland ancestors who fought clan against clan) had attacked the boys of this school and had fought them. James, whose father was a stonemason and whose mother was a Highland lassie born near Loch Lomond, was the leader in these battles, but all the fighting was forgotten when he heard that a boy was in danger of his life, and so he had plunged in as swiftly to save him as he would have done for any boy from his own school.

We do not hear that James was clever at lessons in his school, but when there was anything to be done, he had the quickest hand, the keenest eye, the swiftest mind, and the most daring heart in all the village.

Though he loved the hills and glens and the mountain torrent, James, above everything else, revelled in the sea. One day a little later on, after the rescue of his friend from drowning, James stood on the quay at Inverary gazing across the loch and watching the sails of the fishing boats, when he heard a loud cry.

He looked round. There, on the edge of the quay, stood a mother wringing her hands and calling out that her child had fallen into the water and was drowning. James ran along the quay, and taking off his coat as he dashed to the spot, he dived into the water and, seizing the little child by the dress, drew him ashore. The child seemed dead, but when they laid him on the quayside, and moved his arms, his breath began to come and go again and the colour returned to his cheeks.

Twice Chalmers had saved others from drowning. Three times he himself, as the result of his daring adventures in the sea, was carried home, supposed to be dead by drowning.

At another time he, with two other boys, thrust a tarred herring-box into the sea from the sandy shore between the two rocky points where the western sea came up the narrow Loch Fyne.

"Look at James!" shouted one of the boys to his companions as Chalmers leapt into the box.

It almost turned over, and he swayed and rolled and then steadied as the box swung out from the shore.

The other boys, laughing and shouting, towed him and his boat through the sea as they walked along the shore. Suddenly, as they talked, they staggered forward. The cord had snapped and they fell on the sand, still laughing, but when they stood up again the laughter died on their lips. James was being swiftly carried out by the current to sea--and in a tarred herring-box! He had no paddle, and his hands were of no effect in trying to move the boat toward the shore.

The boys shouted. There came an answering cry from the door of a cottage in the village. A fisherman came swinging down the beach, strode to his boat, took the two boys into it, and taking an oar himself and giving the other to the two boys, they pulled out with the tide. They reached James and rescued him just as the herring-box was sinking. He went home to the little cottage where he lived, and his mother gave him a proper thrashing.

Some of James' schoolfellows used to go on Sundays to a school in Inverary. He made up his mind to join them. The class met in the vestry of the United Presbyterian Church there. After their lesson they went together into the church to hear a closing address. Mr. Meikle, the minister, who was also superintendent of the school, one afternoon took from his pocket a magazine (a copy of the "Presbyterian Record"). From this magazine he read a letter from a brave missionary in the far-off cannibal islands of Fiji. The letter told of the savage life there and of how, already, the story of Jesus was leading the men no longer to drag their victims to the cannibal ovens, nor to pile up the skulls of their enemies so as to show their own bravery. The writer said they were beginning happier lives in which the awful terror of the javelin and the club, and the horror of demons and witches was gone.

When Mr. Meikle had finished reading the magazine he folded it up again and then looked round on all the boys in the school, saying:

"I wonder if there is a boy here this afternoon who will become a missionary, and by and by bring the Gospel to other such cannibals as those?"

Even as the minister said those words, the adventurous heart of young Chalmers leapt in reply as he said to himself, "Yes, God helping me, I will."

He was just a freckled, dark-haired boy with hazel eyes, a boy tingling with the joy of the open air and with the love of the heave and flow of the sea. But when he made up his mind to do a thing, however great the difficulties or dangers, James usually carried it through.

So it came about that some years later in 1866, having been trained and accepted by the London Missionary Society, Chalmers, as a young man, walked across the gangway to a fine new British-built clipper ship. It had been christened John Williams after the great hero missionary[34] who gave up his life on the beach of Erromanga.

This boy, who loved the sea and breathed deep with joy in the face of adventure and peril, had set his face towards the deep, long breakers of the far-off Pacific. He was going to carry to the South Seas the story of the Hero and Saviour Whom he had learnt to love within the sound of the Atlantic breakers that dashed and fretted against the rocks of Western Scotland.

FOOTNOTES:

[Footnote 34: See Chapter VII.]

CHAPTER XIII

THE SCOUT OF PAPUA[35]

Chalmers, the Friend

(Date of Incident, about 1893)

The quick puffing of the steam launch Miro was the only sound to break the stillness of the mysterious Aivai[36] River. On the launch were three white people--two men and a woman. They were the first who had ever broken the silence of that stream.

They gazed out under the morning sun along the dead level of the Purari[37] delta, for they had left behind them the rolling breakers of the Gulf of Papua in order to explore this dark river. Away to the south rolled the blue waters between this vast island of New Guinea and Northern Australia.

They saw on either bank the wild tangle of twisted mangroves with their roots higher than a man, twined together like writhing serpents. They peered through the thick bush with its green leaves drooping down to the very water's edge. But mostly they looked ahead over the bow of the boat along the green-brown water that lay ahead of them, dappled with sunlight under the trees. For they were facing an unknown district where savage Papuans lived--as wild as hawks. They did not know what adventure might meet them at the next bend of the river.

"Splendid! Splendid!" cried one of the white men, a bearded giant whose flashing eyes and mass of brown hair gave him the look of a lion. "We will make it the white woman's peace. Bravo!" And he turned to Mrs. Abel, whose face lit up with pleasure at his happy excitement.

"No white man has even seen the people of Iala,"[38] said Tamate--for that was the native name given to James Chalmers, the Scottish boy who had now gone out to far-off Papua as a missionary.[39] "Iko there"--and he pointed to a stalwart Papuan who stood by the funnel--"is the only one of us who has seen them and can speak their tongue.

"It is dangerous for your wife to go among these people," he went on, turning to Mr. Abel, "but she will help us more than anything else possibly can to make friends." And Mr. Abel nodded, for he knew that when the Papuans mean to fight they send their women and children away; and that when they saw Mrs. Abel they would believe that the white people came as friends and not enemies.

As the steamer carried this scouting party against the swift current up the river toward Iala, Tamate wanted to find how far up the river the village lay. So he beckoned Iko to him. Tamate did not know a word of the dialect which Iko spoke, but he had with him an old wrinkled Papuan, who knew Iko's language, and who looked out with worshipping eyes at the great white man who was his friend. So Tamate, wishing to ask Iko how far away the village of Iala was, spoke first to old Vaaburi,[40] and then Vaaburi asked Iko.

Iko stretched out his dark forefinger, and made them understand that that finger meant the length of their journey to Iala. Then with his other hand he touched his forefinger under the second joint to show how far they had travelled on their journey--not a third of the distance.

Hour after hour went by, as the steamer drove her way through the swiftly running waters of Aivai. And ever Iko pointed further and further up his finger until at last they had reached his claw-like nail. By three o'clock the middle of the nail was reached. The eyes of all looked anxiously ahead. At every curve of the river they strained their sight to see if Iala were in view. How would these savage people welcome the white men and woman in their snorting great canoe that had no paddles, nor oars? There came a sharp bend in the river, and then a long straight reach of water lying between the forest-covered banks. Suddenly Iko called out, and Tamate and Mr. and Mrs. Abel peered ahead.

The great trees of the river nearly met above their heads, and only a narrow strip of sky could be seen.

There in the distance were the houses of Iala, close clustered on both banks of the steaming river. They stood on piles of wood driven into the mud, like houses on stilts, and their high-pointed bamboo roofs stood out over the river like gigantic poke-bonnets.

"Slow," shouted Tamate to the engineer. The Miro slackened speed till she just stemmed the running current and no more.

"It will be a bit of a shock to them," said Tamate to his friends, "to see this launch. We will give them time to get their wits together again."

Looking ahead through their glasses, the white men and Mrs. Abel could see canoes swiftly crossing and re-crossing the river and men rushing about.

"Full speed ahead," cried Tamate again, and then after a few revolutions of the engine, "Go slow. It will never do," he said, "to drop amongst them while they are in that state. They will settle down presently." And then, as he looked up at the sky between the waving branches of the giant trees, "we have got a good two hours' daylight yet," he said.

Life and death to Tamate and his friends hung in the balance, for they were three people unarmed, and here were dark savage warriors in hundreds. Everything depended on his choosing just the right moment for going into the midst of these people. So he watched them closely, knitting his shaggy eyebrows together as he measured their state of mind by their actions. He was the Scout of Christ in Papua, and he must be watchful and note all those things that escape most men but mean so much to trained eyes. Tamate seemed to have a strange gift that made him able, even where other men could tell nothing, to say exactly when it was, and when it was not, possible to go among a wild, untouched tribe.

Now the bewildered Ialan savages had grown quieter. Tamate called to the engineer to drive ahead once more. Slowly the launch forged her way through the running waters and drew nearer and nearer to the centre of Iala.

There on either side stood the houses in long rows stretching up the river, and on the banks hundreds of men stood silent and as still as trees. Their canoes lay half in and half out of the water ready for instant launching. In each canoe stood its crew erect and waiting. All the women and children had been sent away, for these men were out to fight. They did not know whether this strange house upon the water with the smoke coming from its chimney was the work of gods or devils. Still they stood there to face the strange thing and, if need be, to fight.

Brown Iko stood in the bows of the _Miro_; near him stood Tamate. Then the engine stopped and the anchor was dropped overboard. The savages stood motionless. Not a weapon could be seen. The engineer, hearing the anchor-chain rattle through the hole, blew the steam-whistle in simple high spirits. As the shriek of the whistle echoed under the arches of the trees, with the swiftness of lightning the Ialan warriors swung their long bows from behind their bodies. Without stooping each caught up an arrow that stood between his toes and with one movement fixed it and pulled the bamboo strings of their black bows till the notch of the arrows touched their ears. A hundred arrows were aimed at the hearts of Tamate and Mr. and Mrs. Abel.

Swiftly Iko stood upon the bulwark of the Miro, and shouted just one word at the top of his voice. It was the Ialan word for "Peace." And again he shouted it, and yet again "Peace, Peace!"

Then he cried out "Pouta!"[41] It was the name of the chief of these savages. They had but to let the arrows from their bows and all would have been over. There was silence. What order would Pouta give?

Then from the bank on their right came the sound of an answering voice. In a flash every arrow was taken from its bow, and again not a weapon was to be seen.

Iko then called out again to Pouta, and Tamate told Iko what he was to say to his friend, the savage chief. For some minutes the conversation went on. At last Iko came to the point of asking for a canoe to take them ashore.

Chief Pouta hesitated. Then he gave his command, and a large canoe was launched from the bank into the river and slowly paddled towards the Miro.

As the canoe came towards them, Tamate turned to Mrs. Abel, who had stood there without flinching with all the arrows pointed toward the boat; and he spoke words like these: "Your bravery is our strength. Seeing you makes them believe that we come for peace. You give them greater confidence in us than all our words."

By this time the canoe had paddled alongside the launch. Tamate went over the side first into the canoe, then Mrs. Abel, then Mr. Abel, Iko, and Vaaburi. The canoe pushed off again and paddled toward the landing place, where a crowd of Ialan savages filled every inch of space.

As soon as the bow of the canoe touched the bank, Tamate, without hesitating a second, stepped out with Iko. Together they walked up to the chief Pouta, and Tamate put his arms around him in an embrace of peace.

Pouta, standing on a high place, shouted to all his warriors. But none of the white people knew a word of his meaning.

Look where they would, in every direction, this white woman and the two men were completely surrounded by an unbroken mass of wild and armed savages, who stood gazing upon the strange apparitions in their midst.

Tamate, without a pause, perfectly calm, and showing no signs of fear, spoke to Pouta and his men through old Vaaburi and Iko.

"We have come," he said, "so that we may be friends. We have come without weapons. We have brought with us a woman of our tribe, for we come in peace. We are strangers. But we come with great things to tell. Some day we will come again and will stay with you and will tell you all our message. To-day we come only to make friends."

Then Iko closed his eyes and prayed in the language of the people of Iala.

Turning to his friends when the prayer was over, Tamate said quietly: "Now, we must get aboard as quickly as we possibly can. My plan for a first visit is to come, make friends and get away again swiftly. When we are gone they will talk to one another about us. Next time we come we shall meet friends."

So they walked down through an avenue of armed Papuans to the bank, and got into the canoe again: the paddles flashed as she drove swiftly through the water toward the launch. As they climbed her side, the anchor was weighed, the Miro swung round, her engines started, and, carried down by the swift stream, she slipped past the packed masses of silent men who lined the banks.

It is a great thing to be a pathfinder through a country which no man has penetrated before. But it is a greater thing to do as these missionary-scouts did on their journey up the Aivai and find a path of friendship into savage lives. To do that was the greatest joy in Tamate's life. For he said, when he had spent many years in this work:

"Recall the twenty-one years, give me back all its experiences, give me its shipwrecks, give me its standings in the face of death, give it me surrounded with savages with spears and clubs, give it me back again with spears flying about me, with the club knocking me to the ground, give it me back, and I will still be your missionary."

FOOTNOTES:

[Footnote 35: Pa-poo-[)a].]

[Footnote 36: A-ee-v[)a]-ee.]

[Footnote 37: Poo-r[)a]-ree.]

[Footnote 38: Ee-[)a]-I[)a].]

[Footnote 39: He had spent some sixteen years in the South Sea Island of Rarotonga and had in 1877 become a pioneer among the cannibals of Papua (New Guinea).]

[Footnote 40: V[=a][=a]-boo-ree.]

[Footnote 41: Poo-o-t[)a].]

CHAPTER XIV

A SOUTH SEA SAMARITAN

Ruatoka (Date of Incident, about 1878)

It was a dark night and silent. The swish and lapping of the waters on the Port Moresby beach on the southern shore of the immense island of New Guinea, filled the air with a quiet hush of expectation.

In a little white house sat a tall, dark man with his wife. The man was Ruatoka. If you had asked "Who is Ruatoka?" of all the Papuans for miles around Port Moresby, they would have wondered at your ignorance. "Ruatoka," they would have told you, was a "Jesus man." He walked among their villages, and did not fear them when they threatened him with spears and clubs. He gave them medicines when they were ill, and nursed them. He spoke strong words to them which made their hearts turn to water within them when he showed that they did wrong. He often stopped them from fighting.

Ruatoka, with his wife, had sailed from the South Sea Islands with Tamate,[42] who was to them their great hero.

"My fathers of old were heathen, savage men on the island of Mangaia," he would say. "The white men came to them and brought the story of Jesus. Now we are happy. But we, too, must go to the men of New Guinea, just as the white men came to us. To-day the New Guinea Papuans are savage cannibals and heathen. To-morrow they will know Jesus and be as happy as we are."

So Ruatoka had been trained as a teacher and preacher as well as a house-builder and carpenter; and his wife was taught how to teach children as well as good housekeeping.

This was the brown man, Ruatoka, who sat that night in his little house at

Port Moresby on the shore behind the great reef of Papua. Suddenly there came a knock at his door. The door opened, and the black, frightened faces of Papuans, with staring eyes, looked at him.

"What is the matter?" he asked.

And they told him that, as they came at sunset along the path from the people of Larogi to Port Moresby, they found by the side of the path a white man. "He was dying," they said. "We were afraid to touch him. If we touched him and he died, his ghost would haunt us for evermore."

Ruatoka stood up at once and reached for his lantern, and turning to the men said:

"Come and guide me to the place."

They said, "No, we are afraid of the demon spirit. It is night. The man will die. We are afraid of the spirits. We will not go."

Ruatoka's father had told him when he was a boy how his own people in the years before had dreaded the spirit-demons of Mangaia, but that he must learn that there were no spirits to be dreaded; that one great Father-Spirit ruled above all, and would take care of His children, and that all those children must love one another.

So Rua, as they called him, knowing that the white man who lay sick by the roadside in the night, though of another colour, was yet a brother, and knowing that no demon spirit could harm him in the dark, lighted his lantern, poured water into a bottle, took a long piece of cloth, folded it up, and started out under the stars.

He walked for mile after mile up steep hills and down into valleys along the path; but nothing did he hear save the cry of a night bird. At last he had gone five miles, and was wondering whether he could ever find the sick man (for the long grass towered up on either side and all was still), when he heard a low moaning. Listening intently he found the direction of the sound, and then moved towards it. He found there, at the side of the path, a white man named Neville, nearly dead. He was moaning with the pain of the fever, yet unconscious.

Taking his bottle, Ruatoka poured a little water down the throat of the man. He then took the long piece of cloth, wound it round Neville, took the two ends in his hands, and stooping, he pulled and strained with all his great strength, until at last Neville lay like a sack upon his shoulders. Staggering along, Ruatoka climbed the hills that rose 300 feet high. Again and again he was bound to rest, for the man on his shoulders was as heavy as Ruatoka himself. He tottered down the hill path, and at last, just as the first light of dawn was breaking over the eastern hills, Ruatoka staggered into his home, laid the sick man upon the only bed he had, and then himself laid down upon the floor, wearied almost to death. There he slept while his wife nursed and tended the fever-stricken Neville back to life.

* * * * *

Over a thousand years before that day Wilfrid[43] had brought life and joy to the starving Saxons of the South coast of England. A hundred years before that day white men, the great-great-grandchildren of those Saxons, had started out in The Duff and, sailing across the world, had taken life and joy in the place of the terror of demons and the death by the club to the men of the Islands of the Seas.

Now Ruatoka, the South Sea islander, having in his heart the same brave spirit of the Good Shepherd--that spirit of the Good Samaritan, of help and preparedness, of courage and of chivalry, had carried life and joy back to the North Sea islander, the Briton who had fallen by the roadside in Papua.

Ruatoka was a brown Greatheart. It was with him as it must be with all brave sons who serve that great Captain, Jesus Christ: he wanted to be in the front of the battle. When the great Tamate was killed and eaten by the cannibals of Goaribari, Ruatoka wrote a letter to a missionary who lived and still lives in Papua. This is the end of the letter:

"Hear my wish. It is a great wish. The remainder of my strength I would spend in the place where Tamate was killed. In that village I would live. In that place where they killed men, Jesus Christ's name and His word I would teach to the people that they may become Jesus' children. My wish is just this.

You know it. I have spoken.

RUATOKA."

FOOTNOTES:

[Footnote 42: James Chalmers: see Chapter XIII.]

[Footnote 43: See Chapter II.]

Book Three: THE PATHFINDERS OF AFRICA

CHAPTER XV

THE MAN WHO WOULD GO ON

David Livingstone (Dates born 1813, died 1873)

There was a deathly stillness in the hot African air as two bronzed Scots strode along the narrow forest path.

The one, a young, keen-eyed doctor,[44] glanced quickly through the trees and occasionally turned aside to pick some strange orchid and to slip it into his collecting case. The other strode steadily along with that curious, "resolute forward tread" of his.[45] He was David Livingstone. Behind them came a string of African bearers carrying in bundles on their heads the tents and food of the explorers.

Suddenly, with a crunch, Livingstone's heel went through a white object half hidden in the long grass--a thing like an ostrich's egg. He stooped--and his strong, bronzed face was twisted with mingled sorrow and anger, as, looking into the face of his younger friend, he gritted out between his clenched teeth, "The slave-raiders again!"

It was the whitening skull of an African boy.

For weeks those two Britons had driven their little steamer (the Asthmatic they called her, because of her wheezing engines) up the Zambesi river and were now exploring its tributary the Shir?

Each morning, before they could start the ship's engines, they had been obliged to take poles and push from between the paddles of the wheels the dead bodies of Africans--men, women, and children--slain bodies which had floated down from the villages that the Arab slave-raiders had burned and sacked. Livingstone was out on the long, bloody trail of the slaver, the trail that stretched on and on into the heart of Africa where no white man had ever been.

This negro boy's skull, whitening on the path, was only one more link in the long, sickening shackle-chain of slavery that girdled down-trodden Africa.

The two men strode on. The forest path opened out to a broad clearing. They were in an African village. But no voice was heard and no step broke the horrible silence. It was a village of death. The sun blazed on the charred heaps which now marked the sites of happy African homes; the gardens were desolate and utterly destroyed. The village was wiped out. Those who had submitted were far away, trudging through the forest, under the lash of the slaver; those who had been too old to walk or too brave to be taken without fight were slain.

The heart of Livingstone burned with one great resolve--he would track this foul thing into the very heart of Africa and then blazon its horrors to the whole world.

The two men trudged back to the river bank again. Now, with their brown companions, they took the shallow boat that they had brought on the deck of the Asthmatic, and headed still farther up the Shir?river from the Zambesi toward the unknown Highlands of Central Africa.

Facing Spears and Arrows Only the sing-song chant of the Africans as they swung their paddles, and the frightened shriek of a glittering parrot, broke the stillness as the boat pushed northward against the river current.

The paddles flashed again, and as the boat came round a curve in the river they were faced by a sight that made every man sit, paddle in hand, motionless with horror. The bank facing them in the next curve of the river was black with men. The ranks of savages bristled with spears and arrows. A chief yelled to them to turn back. Then a cloud of arrows flew over the boat.

"Go on," said Livingstone quietly to the Africans. Their paddles took the water and the boat leapt toward the savage semi-circle on the bank. The water was shallower now. Before any one realised what was happening Livingstone had swung over the edge of the boat and, up to his waist in water, was wading ashore with his arms above his head.

"It is peace!" he called out, and waded on toward the barbs of a hundred arrows and spears. The men in the boat sat breathless, waiting to see their leader fall with a score of spears through his body. But the savages on the bank were transfixed with amazement at Livingstone's sheer audacity. Awed by something god-like in this unflinching and unarmed courage, no finger let fly a single arrow.

"You think," he called to the chief, "that I am a slave-raider." For Livingstone knew that he had never in all his wanderings been attacked by Africans save where they had first been infuriated by the cruel raiders.

The chief scowled.

"See," cried Livingstone, baring his arm to show his white skin as he again and again had done when threatened by Africans, "is this the colour of the men who come to make slaves and to kill?"

The savages gazed with astonishment. They had never before seen so white a skin.

"No," Livingstone went on, "this is the skin of the tribe that has heart toward the African."

Almost unconsciously the man had dropped the spear points and arrow heads as he was speaking. The chief listened while Livingstone, who was now on the bank, told the savages how he had come across the great waters from a far-off land with a message of peace and goodwill.

Unarmed and with a dauntless heroism the "white man who would go on" had won a great victory over that tribe. He now passed on in his boat up the river and over rapids toward the wonderful shining Highlands in the heart of Africa.

"Deliverance to the Captives"

Dr. Kirk was recalled to England by the British Government; but Livingstone trudged on in increasing loneliness over mountains and across rivers and lakes, plunging through marshes, racked a score of times with fever, robbed of his medicines, threatened again and again by the guns of the slave-raiding Arabs and the spears and clubs of savage head-hunters, bearing on his bent shoulders the Cross of the negroes' agony--slavery, till at last, alone and on his knees in the dead of night, our Greatheart crossed his last River, into the presence of his Father in heaven.

Yet still, though his body was dead, his spirit would go on. For the life Livingstone lived, the death he died, and the record he wrote of the slave-raiders' horrible cruelties thrilled all Britain to heal that "open sore of the world." Queen Victoria made Dr. Kirk her consul at Zanzibar, and told him to make the Sultan of Zanzibar order all slave-trading through that great market to cease. And to-day, because of David Livingstone, through all the thousands of miles of Africa over which he trod, no man dare lay the shackles of slavery on another. To-day, where Livingstone saw the slave-market in Zanzibar, a grand church stands, built by negro hands, and in that cathedral you may hear the negro clergy reading such words as--

"The voice of one crying in the wilderness, Prepare ye the way of the Lord, Make His paths straight,"

and African boys singing in their own tongue words that sum up the whole life of David Livingstone.

"He hath sent me to heal the broken-hearted, To preach deliverance to the captives."

FOOTNOTES:

[Footnote 44: Dr Kirk, now Sir John Kirk, G.C.M.G., who, leaning upon his

African ebony stick and gazing with his now dimmed eyes into the glow of the fire, told me many stories of his adventures with Livingstone on his Zambesi journeyings, including this one. See next chapter.]

[Footnote 45: A friend of mine asked a very old African in Matabeleland whether--as a boy--he remembered Dr. Livingstone. "Oh, yes," replied the aged Matabele, "he came into our village out of the bush walking thus," and the old man got up and stumped along, imitating the determined tread of Livingstone, which, after sixty years, was the one thing he remembered.]

CHAPTER XVI

THE BLACK PRINCE OF AFRICA

Khama (Dates 1850--the present day)

One day men came running into a village in South Africa to say that a strange man, whose body was covered with clothes and whose face was not black, was walking toward their homes. He was coming from the South.

Never before had such a man been seen in their tribe. So there was great excitement and a mighty chattering went through the round wattle of mud huts with their circular thatched roofs.

The African Chief, Sekhome--who was the head of this Bamangwato tribe and who was also a noted witch-doctor--started out along the southward trail to meet the white man. By his side ran his eldest son. He was a lithe, blithe boy; his chocolate coloured skin shone and the muscles rippled as he trotted along. He was so swift that his name was the name of the antelope that gallops across the veldt. Cama is what the Bamangwato call the antelope. Khama is how we spell the boy's name.

He gazed in wonder as he saw a sturdy man wearing clothes such as he had not seen before--what we call coat and hat, trousers and boots. He looked into the bronzed face of the white man and saw that his eyes and mouth were kind. Together they walked back into the village. Chief Sekhome found that the white man's name was David Livingstone; and that he was a kind doctor who could make boys and men better when they were ill, with medicines out of a black japanned box.

When evening came the boy Khama saw the strange white man open another box and take out a curious thing which seemed to open yet was full of hundreds and hundreds of leaves. Khama had never seen such a thing in his life and he could not understand why Livingstone opened it and kept looking at it for a long time, for he had never seen a book before and did not even know what letters were or what reading was.

It seemed wonderful to him when he heard that that book could speak to Livingstone without making any sound and that it told him about the One Infinite, Holy, Loving God, Who is Father of all men, black or brown or white, and Whose Son, Jesus Christ, came to teach us all to love God and to love one another. For the book was the Bible which Livingstone all through his heroic exploring of Africa read each day.

So Livingstone passed on from the village; but this boy Khama never forgot him, and in time--as we shall see--other white men came and taught Khama himself to read that same book and worship that same God.

The Fight with the Lion Meanwhile strange adventures came to the growing young Khama. This is the story of some of them:

The leaping flames of a hunting camp-fire threw upon the dark background of thorn trees weird shadows of the men who squatted in a circle on the ground, talking.

The men were all Africans, the picked hunters from the tribe of the Bamangwato. They were out on the spoor of a great lion that had made himself the terror of the tribe. Night after night the lion had leapt among their oxen and had slain the choicest in the chief's herds. Again and again the hunters had gone out on the trail of the ferocious beast; but always they returned empty-handed, though boasting loudly of what they would do when they should face the lion.

"To-morrow, yes, to-morrow," cried a young Bamangwato hunter rolling his eyes, "I will slay _tau e bogale_--the fierce lion."

The voices of the men rose on the night air as the whole group declared that the beast should ravage their herds no more--the whole group, except one. This young man's tense face and the keen eyes that glowed in the firelight showed his contempt for those who swaggered so much and did so little. He was Khama, the son of Sekhome, the chief. The wild flames gleamed on him as he stood there, full six feet of tireless manhood leaning on his gun, like a superb statue carved in ebony. Those swift, spare limbs of his, that could keep pace with a galloping horse, gave him the right to his name, Khama--the Antelope.

The voices dropped, and the men, rolling themselves in the skins of wild beasts, lay down and slept--all except one, whose eyes watched in the darkness as sleeplessly as the stars. When they were asleep Khama took up his gun and went out into the starry night.

The night passed. As the first flush of dawn paled the stars, and the men around the cold ashes of the fire sat up, they gazed in awed amazement. For they saw, striding toward them, their tall young chieftain; and over his shoulders hung the tawny skin and mane of a full-grown king lion. Alone in the night he had slain the terror of the tribe!

The men who had boasted of what they meant to do and had never performed, never heard Khama--either at that time or later--make any mention of this great feat.

It was no wonder that the great Bamangwato tribe looked at the tall, silent, resolute young chieftain and, comparing him with his crafty father Sekhome and his treacherous, cowardly younger brother Khamane, said, "Khama is our _boikanyo_--our confidence."

The Fight with the Witch-doctors

The years went by; and that fierce old villain Sekhome plotted and laid ambush against the life of his valiant son, Khama. Men who followed David Livingstone into Africa had come as missionaries to his tribe and had taught him the story of Jesus and given him the knowledge of reading and writing. So Khama had become a Christian, though Sekhome his father was still a heathen witch-doctor. Khama would have nothing to do with the horrible ceremonies by which the boys of the tribe were initiated into manhood; nor would he look on the heathen rain-making incantations, though his father smoked with anger against him. Under a thousand insults and threats of death Khama stood silent, never insulting nor answering again, and always treating with respect his unnatural father.

"You, as the son of a great chief, must marry other wives," said old Sekhome, whose wives could not be numbered. Young Khama firmly refused, for the Word of God which ruled his life told him that he must have but one wife. Sekhome foamed with futile rage.

"You must call in the rain-doctors to make rain," said Sekhome, as the parched earth cracked under the flaming sun. Khama knew that their wild incantations had no power to make rain, but that God alone ruled the heavens. So he refused.

Sekhome now made his last and most fearful attack. He was a witch-doctor and master of the witch-doctors whose ghoulish incantations made the Bamangwato tremble in terror of unseen devils.

One night the persecuted Khama woke at the sound of strange clashing and chanting. Looking out he saw the fitful flame of a fire. Going out from his hut, he saw the lolwapa or court in front of it lit up with weird flames round which the black wizards danced with horns and lions' teeth clashing about their necks, and with manes of beasts' hair waving above their horrible faces. As they danced they cast charms into the fire and chanted loathsome spells and terrible curses on Khama. As a boy he had been taught that these witch-doctors had the power to slay or to smite with foul diseases. He would have been more than human if he had not felt a shiver of nameless dread at this lurid and horrible dance of death.

Yet he never hesitated. He strode forward swiftly, anger and contempt on his face, scattering the witch-doctors from his path and leaping full upon their fire of charms, stamped it out and scattered its embers broadcast. The wizards fled into the darkness of the night.

The Fight with the Kaffir Beer At last Khama's treacherous old father, Sekhome, died. Khama was acclaimed the supreme chief of all the

Bamangwato.[46] He galloped out at the head of his horsemen to pursue Lobengula, the ferocious chief of the Matabele who had struck fear into the Bamangwato for many years. Even Lobengula, who to his dying day carried in his neck a bullet from Khama's gun, said of him, "The Bamangwato are dogs, but Khama is a man."

Khama had now freed his people from the terror of the lion, the tyranny of witch-doctors, and the dread of the Matabele. Yet the deadliest enemy of Khama and the most loathsome tyrant of the Bamangwato was still in power,--the strong drink which degrades the African to unspeakable depths.

Even as Khama charged at the head of his men into the breaking ranks of the Matabele, his younger brother, Khamane, whom he had put in charge of his city in his absence, said to the people: "You may brew beer again now." Many of the people did not obey, but others took the corn of the tribe and brewed beer from it.

At night the cries of beaten women rose, and the weird chants of incantations and of foul unclean dances were heard. Khamane called the older men together around his fire. Pots of beer passed from hand to hand. As the men grew fuddled they became bolder and more boastful. Khamane then spoke to them and said, "Why should Khama rule you? Remember he forbids you to make and to drink beer. He has done away with the dances of the young men. He will not let you make charms or throw enchanted dice or make incantations for rain. He is a Christian. If I ruled you, you should do all these things."

When Khama rode back again into his town he saw men and women lying drunk under the eaves of their huts and others reeling along the road. At night the sounds of chants and drinking dances rose on the air.

His anger was terrible. For once he lost his temper. He seized a burning torch and running to the hut of Khamane set fire to the roof and burned the house down over his drunken brother's head. He ordered all the beer that had been brewed to be seized, and poured it out upon the veldt. He knew that he was fighting a fiercer enemy than the Matabele, a foe that would throttle his tribe and destroy all his people if he did not conquer it. The old men of the tribe muttered against him and plotted his death. He met them face to face. His eyes flashed.

"When I was still a lad," he said, "I used to think how I would govern my town and what kind of a kingdom it should be. One thing I determined, I would not rule over a drunken town or people. I WILL NOT HAVE DRINK IN THIS TOWN. If you must have it you must go."

The Fight with the White Man's "Fire-water"

Khama had conquered for the moment. But white men, Englishmen, came to the town. They set up stores. And in the stores they began to sell brandy from large casks.

The drinking of spirits has more terrible effects on the African than even on white men. Once he starts drinking, the African cannot stop and is turned into a sot. The ships of the white man have been responsible to a terrible extent for sending out the "fire-water" to Africa.

Khama called the white traders in the tribe together.

"It is my desire," he said, "that no strong drink shall be sold in my town."

"We will not bring the great casks of brandy," they replied, "but we hope you will allow us to have cases of bottles as they are for medicine."

"I consent," said Khama, "but there must be no drunkenness."

"Certainly," the white men replied, "there shall be no drunkenness."

In a few days one of the white traders had locked himself into his house in drunken delirium, naked and raving. Morning after morning Khama rose before daybreak to try and get to the man when he was sober, but all the time he was drunk. Then one morning this man gathered other white men together in a house and they sat drinking and then started fighting one another.

A boy ran to Khama to tell him. The chief went to the house and strode in. The room was a wreck. The men lay senseless with their white shirts stained with blood.

Khama with set, stern face turned and walked to the house where he often went for counsel, the home of his friend, Mr. Hepburn, the missionary. Mr. Hepburn lay ill with fever. Khama told him what the white men had done. Hepburn burned with shame and anger that his own fellow-countrymen should so disgrace themselves. Ill as he was he rose and went out with the chief and saw with his own eyes that it was as Khama said.

"I will clear them all out of my town," cried the chief.

It was Saturday night.

Khama's Decisive Hour

On the Monday morning Khama sent word to all the white men to come to him. It was a cold, dreary day. The chief sat waiting in the _Kgotla_[47] while the white men came together before him. Hepburn, the missionary, sat by his side. Those who knew Khama saw as soon as they looked into his grim face that no will on earth could turn him from his decisions that day.

"You white men,"[48] he said to them sternly, "have insulted and despised me in my own town because I am a black man. If you despise us black men, what do you want here in the country that God has given to us? Go back to your own country."

His voice became hard with a tragic sternness.

"I am trying," he went on, "to lead my people to act according to the word of God which we have received from you white people, and yet you show them an example of wickedness such as we never knew. You," and his voice rose in burning scorn, "you, the people of the word of God! You know that some of my own brothers"--he was referring to Khamane especially--"have learned to like the drink, and you know that I do not want them to see it even, that they may forget the habit. Yet you not only bring it in and offer it to them, but you try to tempt me with it.

"I make an end of it to-day. Go! Take your cattle and leave my town and never come back again!"

No man moved or spoke. They were utterly shamed and bewildered. Then one white man, who had lived in the town since he was a lad, pleaded with Khama for pity as an old friend.

"You," said the chief with biting irony, "my friend? You--the ringleader of those who despise my laws. You are my worst enemy. You pray for pity? No! for you I have no pity. It is my duty to have pity on my people over whom God placed me, and I am going to show them pity to-day; and that is my duty to them and to God.... Go!"

And they all went.

Then the chief ordered in his young warriors and huntsmen.

"No one of you," he said, "is to drink beer." Then he called a great meeting of the whole town. In serried masses thousand upon thousand the Bamangwato faced their great chief. He lifted up his voice:

"I, Khama, your chief, order that you shall not make beer. You take the corn that God has given to us in answer to our prayers and you destroy it. Nay, you not only destroy it, but you make stuff with it that causes mischief among you."

There was some murmuring.

His eyes flashed like steel.

"You can kill me," he said, "but you cannot conquer me."

* * * * *

The Black Prince of Eighty If you rode as a guest toward Khama's town over seventy years after those far-off days when Livingstone first went there, as you came in sight of the great stone church that the chief has built, you would see tearing across the African plain a whirlwind of dust. It would race toward you, with the soft thunder of hoofs in the loose soil. When the horses were almost upon you--with a hand of steel--chief Khama would rein in his charger and his bodyguard would pull up behind him.

Over eighty years old, grey and wrinkled, he would spring from his horse, without help, to greet you--still Khama, the Antelope. Old as he is, he is as alert as ever. He heard that a great all Africa aeroplane route was planned after the Great War. At once he offered to make a great aerodrome, and the day at last came when Khama--eighty-five years old--who had seen Livingstone, the first white man to visit his tribe--stood watching the first aeroplane come bringing a young officer from the clouds.

He stands there, the splendid chief of the Bamangwato--"steel-true, blade-straight." He is the Black Prince of Africa--who has indeed won his spurs against the enemies of his people.

And if you were to ask him the secret of the power by which he has done these things, Khama the silent, who is not used to boasting, would no doubt lead you at dawn to the Kgotla before his huts. There at every sunrise he gathers his people together for their morning prayers at the feet of the Father of our Lord Jesus Christ, the Captain and King of our Great Crusade for the saving of Africa.

FOOTNOTES:

[Footnote 46: In 1875.]

[Footnote 47: The chiefs open-air enclosure for official meetings.]

[Footnote 48: These are Khama's own words taken down at the time by Hepburn.]

CHAPTER XVII

THE KNIGHT OF THE SLAVE GIRLS

George Grenfell (Dates, b. 1849, d. 1906)

The Building of the Steamship When David Livingstone lay dying in his hastily-built hut, in the heart of Africa, with his black companions Susi and Chumah attending him, almost his last words were, "How far away is the Luapula?"

He knew that the river to which the Africans gave that name was only a short distance away and that it flowed northward. He thought that it might be the upper reaches of the Nile, which had been sought by men through thousands of years, but which none had ever explored.

Livingstone died in that hut (1873) and never knew what Stanley, following in his footsteps, discovered later (1876-7), viz., that the Luapula was really the upper stretch of the Congo, the second largest river in the world (3000 miles long), flowing into the Atlantic. The basin of the Congo would cover the whole of Europe from the Black Sea to the English Channel.

In the year when Livingstone died, and before Stanley started to explore the Congo, a young man, who had been thrilled by reading the travels of Livingstone, sailed to the West Coast of Africa to the Kameruns.

His name was George Grenfell, a Cornish boy (born at Sancreed, four miles from Penzance, in England), who was brought up in Birmingham. He was apprenticed at fifteen to a firm of hardware and machinery dealers. Here he picked up, as a lad, some knowledge of machinery that helped him later on the Congo. He had been thrilled to meet at Bristol College, where he was trained for his missionary work, a thin, worn, heroic man of tried steel, Alfred Saker, the great Kamerun missionary, and Grenfell leapt for joy to go out to the dangerous West Coast of Africa, where he worked hard, teaching the Africans to make tables and bricks and to print and read, healing them and preaching to them.

When Stanley came down the Congo to the sea and electrified the world by the story of the great river, Grenfell and the Baptist Missionary Society which he served conceived the daring and splendid plan of starting a chain of mission stations right from the mouth of the Congo eastward across Africa. In 1878 Grenfell was on his way up the river--travelling along narrow paths flanked by grass often fifteen feet high, and crossing swamps and rivers, till after thirteen attempts and in eighteen months he reached Stanley Pool, February 1881. A thousand miles of river lay between Stanley Pool and

Stanley Falls, and even above Stanley Falls lay thirteen hundred miles of navigable river. Canoes were perilous. Hippopotami upset them, and men were dragged down and eaten by crocodiles. They must have a steamer right up there beyond the Falls in the very heart of Africa.

Grenfell went home to England, and the steamer Peace was built on the Thames, Grenfell watching everything being made from the crank to the funnel. She was built, launched, and tried on the Thames; then taken to pieces and packed in 800 packages, weighing 65 lbs. each, and taken to the mouth of the Congo. On the heads and shoulders of a thousand men the whole ship and the food of the party were carried past the rapids, over a thousand miles along narrow paths, in peril of snakes and leopards and enemy savages, over streams crossed by bridges of vine-creepers, through swamps, across ravines.

Grenfell's engineer, who was to have put the ship together, died. At last they reached Stanley Pool. Grenfell with eight negroes started to try to build the ship. It was a tremendous task. Grenfell said the Peace was "prayed together." It was prayer and hard work and gumption. At last the ship was launched, steam was up, the Peace began to move. "She lives, master, she lives!" shouted the excited Africans.

A thousand thrilling adventures came to him as he steamed up and down the river, teaching and preaching, often in the face of poisoned arrows and spears. We are now going to hear the story of one adventure.

The Steamer's Journey

The crocodiles drowsily dosing in the slime of the Congo river bank stirred uneasily as a strange sound broke the silence of the blazing African morning. They lifted their heavy jaws and swung their heads down stream. Their beady eyes caught sight of a Thing mightier than a thousand crocodiles. It was pushing its way slowly up stream.

The sound was the throb of the screw of the steamer from whose funnel a light ribbon of smoke floated across the river. An awning shaded the whole deck from bow to stern. On the top of the awning, under a little square canopy, stood a tall young negro; the muscles in his sturdy arms and his broad shoulders rippled under his dark skin as the wheel swung round in his swift, strong hands.

The steamer drove up stream while the crocodiles, startled by the wash of the boat, slid sullenly down the bank and dived.

A short, bearded man, dressed in white duck, stood on deck at the bows, where the steamer's name, Peace, was painted. He was George Grenfell. His keen eyes gleamed through the spectacles that rested on his strong, arched nose. By his side stood his wife, looking out up the river. They were searching for the landing-place and the hut-roofs of some friendly river-side town.

At last as the bows swung round the next bend in the river they saw a village. The Africans rushed to the bank and hurriedly pushed out their tree-trunk canoes. Grenfell shouted an order. A bell rang. The screw stopped and the steamer lay-to while he climbed down into the ship's canoe and was paddled ashore. The wondering people pushed and jostled around them to see this strange man with his white face.

The Slave Girls As they walked up among the huts, speaking with the men of the town, Grenfell came to an open space. As his quick eyes looked about he saw two little girls standing bound with cords. They were tethered like goats to a stake. Their little faces and round eyes looked all forlorn. Even the wonder of the strange bearded white man hardly kept back the tears that filled their eyes.

"What are these?" he asked, turning to the chief.

The African pointed up the river. Grenfell's heart burned in him, as the chief told how he and his men had swept up the river in their canoes armed with their spears and bows and arrows and had raided another tribe.

"And these," said the chief, pointing to the girls, who began to wonder what was going to happen, "these are two girls that we captured. They are some of our booty. They are slaves. They are tied there till someone will come and buy them."

Grenfell could not resist the silent call of their woeful faces. Quickly he gave beads and cloth to the chief, and took the little girls back with him down to the river bank. As they jumped into the canoe to go aboard the S.S. Peace, the two girls wondered what this strange new master would do with them. Would he be cruel? Yet his eyes looked kind through those funny, round, shining things balanced on his nose.

The girls at once forgot all their sorrows when they jumped on board this wonderful river monster. They felt it shiver and throb and begin to move. The bank went farther and farther away. The Peace had again started up stream.

The girls stood in wonder and gazed with open eyes as the banks slid past. They saw the birds all green and red flashing along the surface of the water, and the huge hippopotami sullenly plunging into the river like the floating islands of earth that sail down the Congo. Their quick eyes noted the quaint iguana, like giant lizards, sunning themselves on the branches of the trees over the stream and then dropping like stones into the stream as the steamer passed.

The Slave Girl's Brother

Then, suddenly, as they came round a bend in the river, all was changed. There ahead Grenfell saw a river town. The canoes were being manned rapidly by warriors. The bank bristled with spears in the hands of ferocious savages, whose faces were made horrible by gashes and loathsome tattooing. In each canoe men stood with bows in their hands and arrows drawn to the head. The throb of the engines ceased. The ship slowed up. But the canoes came on.

The men of this Congo town only knew one thing. Enemies had, only a few weeks earlier, come from down-river, had raided their town, burned their huts, killed many of their braves, and carried away their children. Here were men who had also come from down the river. They must, therefore, be enemies.

Their chief shouted an order. In an instant a score of spears hurtled at the ship and rattled on the steel screens around the deck. The yell of the battle-cry of the tribe echoed and re-echoed down the river.

Grenfell was standing by the little girls. Suddenly one of them with dancing eyes shouted and waved her arms.

"What is it?" cried Grenfell to her.

"See--see!" she cried, pointing to a warrior in a canoe who was just poising a spear, "that is my brother! That is my brother! This is my town!"

"Call to him," said Grenfell.

Her thin childish voice rang out. But no one heard it among the warriors. Again she cried out to her brother. The only answer was a hail of spears and arrows.

Grenfell turned rapidly and shouted an order to the engineer. Instantly a shriek, more wild and piercing than the combined yells of the whole tribe, rent the air. Again the shriek went up. The warriors stood transfixed with spear and arrow in hand like statues in ebony. There was a moment's intense and awful silence. They had never before heard the whistle of a steamer!

"Shout again--quickly," whispered Grenfell to the little African girl.

In a second the child's shrill voice rang out in the silence across the water, crying first her brother's name, and then her own.

The astonished warrior dropped his spear, caught up his paddle and--in a few swift strokes--drove his canoe towards the steamer. His astonishment at seeing his sister aboard overcame all his dread of this shrieking, floating island that moved without sails or paddles.

Quickly she told her story of how the strange white man in the great canoe that smoked had found her in the village of their enemies, had saved her from slavery, and--now, had brought her safely home again. The story passed from lip to lip. Every spear and bow and arrow was dropped.

The girls were quickly put ashore, and as Grenfell walked up the village street every warrior who had but a few moments before been seeking his blood was now gazing at this strange friend who had brought back to the tribe the daughters whom they thought they had lost for ever.

Grenfell went on with his work in face of fever, inter-tribal fighting, slave-raiders, the horrors of wife and slave-slaughter at funerals, witch-killing--and in some ways worse still, the horrible cruelties of the Belgian rubber-traders--for over a quarter of a century.

In June 1906, accompanied by his negro companions, he lay at Yalemba, sick with fever. Two of the Africans wrote a letter for help to other missionaries:

"We are very sorrow," they wrote, "because out Master is very sick. So now we beging you one of you let him come to help Mr Grenfell please. We think now is near to die, but we don't know how to do with him. Yours,

DISASI MAKULO, MASCOO LUVUSU."

To-day all up the fifteen hundred miles of Congo waterway the power of the work done by Grenfell and the men who came with him and after him has changed all the life. Gone are the slave-raiders, the inter-tribal wars, the cruelties of the white men, along that line. There stand instead negroes who cap make bricks, build houses, turn a lathe; engineers, printers, bookbinders, blacksmiths, carpenters, worshipping in churches built with their own hands. But beyond, and among the myriad tributaries and the vast forests millions of men have never yet even heard of the love of God in Jesus Christ, and still work their hideous cruelties.

So Grenfell, like Livingstone, opened a door. It stands open.

CHAPTER XVIII

"A MAN WHO CAN TURN HIS HAND TO ANYTHING"

Alexander Mackay (Dates 1863-1876)

The inquisitive village folk stared over their garden gates at Mr. Mackay, the minister of the Free Kirk of Rhynie, a small Aberdeenshire village, as he stood with his thirteen-year-old boy gazing into the road at their feet. The father was apparently scratching at the stones and dust with his stick. The villagers shook their heads.

"Fat's the minister glowerin' at, wi' his loon Alic, among the stoor o' the turnpike?"[49] asked the villagers of one another.

The minister certainly was powerful in the pulpit, but his ways were more than they could understand. He was for ever hammering at the rocks on the moor and lugging ugly lumps of useless stone homeward, containing "fossils" as he called them.

Now Mr. Mackay was standing looking as though he were trying to find something that he had lost in the road. If they had been near enough to Alec and his father they would have heard words like these:

"You see, Alec, this is the Zambesi River running down from the heart of Africa into the Indian Ocean, and here running into the Zambesi from the north is a tributary, the Shir? Livingstone going up that river found wild savages who ..."

So the father was tracing in the dust of the road with the point of his stick the course of the Zambesi which Livingstone had just explored for the first time.

On these walks with his father Alec, with his blue eyes wide open, used to listen to stories like the Yarn we have read of the marvellous adventures of Livingstone.[50] Sometimes Mr. Mackay would stop and draw triangles and circles with his stick. Then Alec would be learning a problem in Euclid on this strange "blackboard" of the road. He learned the Euclid--but he preferred the Zambesi and Livingstone!

One day Alec was off by himself trudging down the road with a fixed purpose in his mind, a purpose that seemed to have nothing in the world to do with either Africa or Euclid. He marched away from his little village of Rhynie, where the burn runs around the foot of the great granite mountain across the strath. He trudged on for four miles. Then he heard a shrill whistle. Would he be late after all? He ran swiftly toward the little railway station. A ribbon of smoke showed over the cutting, away to the right. Alec entered the station and ran to one end of the platform as the train slowed down and the engine stopped just opposite where he stood.

He gazed at the driver and his mate on the footplate. He followed every movement as the driver came round the engine with his long-nosed oil-can, and opened and shut small brass lids and felt the bearings with his hand to see whether they were hot. The guard waved his green flag. The whistle of the engine shrieked, and the train steamed out of the station along the burnside toward Huntly. Alec gazed down the line till the train was out of sight and then, turning, left the station and trudged homeward. When he reached Rhynie he had walked eight miles to look at a railway engine for two and a half minutes--and he was happy!

As he went along the village street he heard a familiar sound.

"Clang-a-clang clang!--ssssssss!" It was irresistible. He stopped, and stepped into the magic cavern of darkness, gleaming with the forge-fire, where George Lobban, the smith, having hammered a glowing horseshoe into shape, gripped it with his pincers and flung it hissing into the water.

Having cracked a joke with the laughing smith, Alec dragged himself away from the smithy, past the green, and looked in at the stable to curry-comb the pony and enjoy feeling the little beast's muzzle nosing in his hand for oats.

He let himself into the manse and ran up to his work-room, where he began to print off some pages that he had set up on his little printing press.

At supper his mother looked sadly at her boy with his dancing eyes as he told her about the wonders of the railway engine. In her heart she wanted him to be a minister. And she did not see any sign that this boy would ever become one: this lad of hers who was always running off from his books to peer into the furnaces of the gas works, or to tease the village carpenter into letting him plane a board, or to sit, with chin in hands and elbows on knees, watching the saddler cutting and padding and stitching his leather, or to creep into the carding-mill--like the Budge and Toddy whose lives he had read--"to see weels go wound."

It was a bitter cold night in the Christmas vacation fourteen years later.[51] Alec Mackay, now a young engineering student, was lost to all sense of time as he read of the hairbreadth escapes and adventures told by the African explorer, Stanley, in his book, How I found Livingstone.

He read these words of Stanley's:

"For four months and four days I lived with Livingstone in the same house, or in the same boat, or in the same tent, and I never found a fault in him.... Each day's life with him added to my admiration for him. His gentleness never forsakes him: his hopefulness never deserts him. His is the Spartan heroism, the inflexibility of the Roman, the enduring resolution of the Anglo-Saxon. The man has conquered me."

Alexander Mackay put down Stanley's book and gazed into the fire. Since the days when he had trudged as a boy down to the station to see the railway engine he had been a schoolboy in the Grammar School at Aberdeen, and a student in Edinburgh, and while there had worked in the great shipbuilding yards at Leith amid the clang and roar of the rivetters and the engine shop. He was now studying in Berlin, drawing the designs of great engines far more wonderful than the railway engine he had almost worshipped as a boy.

On the desk at Mackay's side lay his diary in which he wrote his thoughts. In that diary were the words that he himself had written:

"This day last year[52] Livingstone died--a Scotsman and a Christian--loving God and his neighbour, in the heart of Africa. 'Go thou and do likewise.'"

Mackay wondered. Could it ever be that he would go into the heart of Africa like Livingstone? it seemed impossible. What was the good of an engineer among the lakes and forests of Central Africa?

On the table by the side of Stanley's How I found Livingstone lay a newspaper, the Edinburgh Daily Review. Mackay glanced at it; then he snatched it up and read eagerly a letter which appeared there. It was a new call to Central Africa--the call, through Stanley, from King M'tesa of Uganda, that home of massacre and torture. These are some of the words that Stanley wrote:

"King M'tesa of Uganda has been asking me about the white man's God....

Oh that some practical missionary would come here. M'tesa would give him anything that he desired--houses, land, cattle, ivory. It is the practical Christian who can ... cure their diseases, build dwellings, teach farming and turn his hand to anything like a sailor--this is the man who is wanted. Such a one, if he can be found, would become the saviour of Africa."

Stanley called for "a practical man who could turn his hand to anything--if he can be found."

The words burned their way into Mackay's very soul.

"If he can be found." Why here, here in this very room he sits--the boy who has worked in the village at the carpenter's bench and the saddler's table, in the smithy and the mill, when his mother wished him to be at his books; the lad who has watched the ships building in the docks of Aberdeen, and has himself with hammer and file and lathe built and made machines in the engineering works--he is here--the "man who can turn his hand to anything." And he had, we remember, already written in his diary:

"Livingstone died--a Scotsman and a Christian--loving God and his neighbour, in the heart of Africa. 'Go thou and do likewise.'"

Mackay did not hesitate. Then and there he took pen and ink and paper and wrote to London to the Church Missionary Society which was offering, in the daily paper that lay before him, to send men out to King M'tesa. The words that Mackay wrote were these:

"My heart burns for the deliverance of Africa, and if you can send me to any one of those regions which Livingstone and Stanley have found to be groaning under the curse of the slave-hunter I shall be very glad."

Within four months Mackay, with some other young missionaries who had volunteered for the same great work, was standing on the deck of the S.S. Peshawur as she steamed out from Southampton for Zanzibar.

He was in the footsteps of Livingstone--"a Scotsman and a Christian"--making for the heart of Africa and "ready to turn his hand to anything" for the sake of Him who as

"... the Carpenter of Nazareth Made common things for God."

FOOTNOTES:

[Footnote 49: "What is the minister gazing at, with his son Alec, in the dust of the road?"]

[Footnote 50: See Chapter XV.]

[Footnote 51: December 12, 1875.]

[Footnote 52: May 1, 1873.]

CHAPTER XIX

THE ROADMAKER

Alexander Mackay (Date, 1878)

After many months of delay at Zanzibar, Mackay with his companions and bearers started on his tramp of hundreds of miles along narrow footpaths, often through swamps, delayed by fierce greedy chiefs who demanded many cloths before they would let the travellers pass. One of the little band of missionaries had already died of fever. When hundreds of miles from the coast, Mackay was stricken with fever and nearly died. His companions sent him back to the coast again to recover, and they themselves went on and put together the Daisy, the boat which the bearers had carried in sections on their heads, on the shore of Victoria Nyanza. So Mackay, racked with fever, was carried back by his Africans over the weary miles through swamp and forest to the coast. At last he was well again, and with infinite labour he cut a great wagon road for 230 miles to Mpapwa. With pick and shovel, axe and saw, they cleared the road of trees for a hundred days.

Mackay wrote home as he sat at night tired by the side of his half-made road, "This will certainly yet be a highway for the King Himself; and all that pass this way will come to know His Name."

At length, after triumphing by sheer skill and will over a thousand difficulties, Mackay reached the southern shore of Victoria Nyanza at Kagei, to find that his surviving companions had gone on to Uganda in an Arab sailing-dhow, leaving on the shore the Daisy, which had been too small to carry them.

On the beach by the side of that great inland sea, Victoria Nyanza, in the heart of Africa, Mackay found the now broken and leaking Daisy. Her cedar planks were twisted and had warped in the blazing sun till every seam gaped. A hippopotamus had crunched her bow between his terrible jaws. Many of her timbers had crumbled before the still greater foe of the African boat-builder--the white ant.

Now, under her shadow lay the man "who could turn his hand to anything," on his back with hammer and chisel in hand. He was rivetting a plate of copper on the hull of the Daisy. Already he had nailed sheets of zinc and lead on stern and bow, and had driven cotton wool picked from the bushes by the lake into the seams to caulk some of the leaks. Around the boat stood crowds of Africans, their dark faces full of astonishment at the white man mending his big canoe.

"Why should a man toil so terribly hard?" they wondered.

The tribesmen of the lake had only canoes hollowed out from a tree-trunk, or made of some planks sewn together with fibres from the banana tree.

At last Mackay had his boat ready to sail up the Victoria Nyanza. The whole of the length of that great sea, itself larger than his own native Scotland, still separated Mackay from the land of Uganda for which he had left Britain over fifteen months earlier.

All through his disappointments and difficulties Mackay fought on. With him, as with Livingstone, nothing had power to break his spirit or quench his burning determination to carry on his God-given plan to serve Africa.

Every use of saw and hammer and chisel, every

"trick of the tool's true trade,"

all the training in the shipbuilding yards and engineering shops at Edinburgh and in Germany helped Mackay to invent some new, daring and ingenious way out of every fresh difficulty.

The Wreck of the "Daisy"

Now at last the Daisy was on the water again; and Mackay and his bearers went aboard[53] and hoisting sail from Kagei ran northward. Before they had gone far black storm clouds swept across the sky. Night fell. Lightning blazed unceasingly and flung up into silhouette the wild outlines of the mountains to the east. The roar of the thunder echoed above the wail of the wind and the threshing of the waves.

All through the dark, Mackay and those of his men who could handle an oar rowed unceasingly. Again and again he threw out his twenty-fathom line, but in vain. He made out a dim line of precipitous cliffs, yet the water seemed fathomless--the only map in existence was a rough one that Stanley had made. At last the lead touched bottom at fourteen fathoms. In the dim light of dawn they rowed and sailed toward a shady beach before the cliffs, and anchored in three and a half fathoms of water.

The storm passed; but the waves from the open sea came roaring in and broke over the Daisy. The bowsprit dipped under the anchor chain, and the whole bulwark on the weatherside was carried away. The next sea swept into the open and now sinking boat. By frantic efforts they heaved up the anchor and the next wave swung the Daisy with a crash onto the beach, where the waves pounded her to a complete wreck, wrenching the planks from the keel. But Mackay and his men managed to rescue her cargo before she went to pieces.

They were wrecked on a shore where Stanley, the great explorer, had years before had a hairbreadth escape from massacre at the hands of the wild savages. But Stanley, living up to the practice he had learned from Livingstone, had turned enemies into friends, and now the natives made no attack on the shipwrecked Mackay.

For eight weeks Mackay laboured there, hard on the edge of the lake, living on the beach in a tent made of spars and sails. With hammer and chisel and saw he worked unsparingly at his task. He cut the middle eight feet from the boat, and bringing her stern and stem together patched the broken ends with wood from the middle part. After two months' work the now dumpier Daisy took the water again, and carried Mackay and his men safely up the long shores of Victoria Nyanza to the goal of all his travelling, the capital of M'tesa, King of Uganda.

The rolling tattoo of goat-skin drums filled the royal reception-hall of King M'tesa, as the great tyrant entered with his chiefs. M'tesa, his dark, cruel heavy face in vivid contrast with his spotless white robe, sat heavily down on his stool of State, while brazen trumpets sent to him from England blared as Mackay entered. The chiefs squatted on low stools and on the rush-strewn mud-floor before the King. At his side stood his Prime Minister, the Katikiro, a smaller man than the King, but swifter and more far-sighted. The Katikiro was dressed in a snowy-white Arab gown covered by a black mantle trimmed with gold. In his hard, guilty face treacherous cunning and masterful cruelty were blended.

M'tesa was gracious to Mackay, and gave him land on which to build his home. More important to Mackay than even his hut was his workshop, where he quickly fixed his forge and anvil, vise and lathe, and grindstone, for he was now in the place where he could practise his skill. It was for this that he had left home and friends, and pressed on in spite of fever and shipwreck to serve Africa and lead her to the worship of Jesus Christ by working and teaching as our Lord did when on earth.

One day the wide thatched roof of that workshop shaded from the flaming rays of the sun a crowded circle of the chiefs of Uganda with their slaves, who loved to come to "hear the bellows roar." They were gazing at Mackay, whose strong, bare right arm was swinging his hammer

"Clang-a-clang-clang."

Then a ruddy glow lit up the dark faces of the watchers and the bronzed face of the white man who in the centre of his workshop was blowing up his forge fire. Gripping in his pincers the iron hoe that was now red-hot, Mackay hammered it into shape and then plunged it all hissing into the bath of water that stood by him.

Hardly had the cloud of steam risen from the bath, when Mackay once more gripped the hoe, and moving to his grindstone placed his foot on the pedal and set the edge of the hoe against the whirling stone. The sparks flew high. A murmur came from the Uganda chiefs who stood around.

"It is witchcraft," they said to one another. "It is witchcraft by which Mazunga-wa-Kazi makes the hard iron tenfold harder in the water. It is witchcraft by which he sends the wheels round and makes our hoes sharp. Surely he is the great wizard."

Mackay caught the sound of the new name that they had given him-- Mazunga-wa-Kazi--the White-Man-at-Work. They called him by this name because to them it was very strange that any man should work with his own hands.

"Women are for work," said the chiefs. "Men go to talk with the King, and to fight and eat."

Mackay paused in his work and turned on them.

"No," he said, "you are wrong. God made man with one stomach and with two hands in order that he may work twice as much as he eats." And Mackay held out before them his own hands blackened with the work of the smithy, rough with the handling of hammer and saw, the file and lathe. "But you," and he turned on them with a laugh and pointed to their sleek bodies as they shone in the glow of the forge fire, "you are all stomach and no hands."

They grinned sheepishly at one another under this attack, and, as Mackay let down the fire and put away his tools, they strolled off to the hill on which the King's beehive-shaped thatched palace was built.

Mackay climbed up the hill on the side of which his workshop stood. From the ridge he gazed over the low-lying marsh from which the women were bearing on their heads the water-pots. He knew that the men and women of the land were suffering from fearful illnesses. He now realised that the fevers came from the poisonous waters of the marsh. He made up his mind how he could help them with his skill. They must have pure water; yet they knew nothing of wells.

Mackay at once searched the hill-side with his spade and found a bed of clay emerging from the side of the hill. He climbed sixteen feet higher up the hill and, bringing the men who could help him together, began digging. He knew that he would reach spring water at the level of the clay, for the rains that had filtered through the earth would stop there.

The Baganda[54] thought that he was mad. "Whoever," they asked one another, "heard of digging in the top of a hill for water?"

"When the hole is so deep," said Mackay, measuring out sixteen feet, "water will come, pure and clean, and you will not need to carry it up the hill from the marsh."

They dug and dug till the hole was too deep to hurl the earth up over the edge. Then Mackay made a pulley, which seemed a magic thing to them, for they could not yet understand the working of wheels; and with rope and bucket the earth was pulled up. Exactly at the depth of sixteen feet the water welled in. The Baganda clapped their hands and danced with delight.

"Mackay is the great wizard. He is the mighty spirit," they cried. "The King must come to see this."

King M'tesa himself wondered at the story of the making of the well and the finding of the water. He gave orders that he was to be carried to view this great wonder. His eyes rolled with astonishment as he saw it and heard of the wonders that were wrought by the work of men.

Yet M'tesa and his men still wondered why any man should work hard. Mackay tried to explain this to the King when he sat in his reception-hall. Work, Mackay told M'tesa, is the noblest thing a man can do, and he told him how Jesus Christ, the Son of the Great Father-Spirit who made all things, did not Himself feel that work was a thing too mean for Him. For our Lord, when He lived on earth at Nazareth, worked with His own hands at the carpenter's bench, and made all labour forever noble.

FOOTNOTES:

CHAPTER XX

FIGHTING THE SLAVE TRADE

Alexander Mackay (Date, 1878)

In the court of King M'tesa, Mackay always saw many boys who used to drive away the flies from the King's face with fans, carry stools for the chiefs and visitors to squat upon, run messages and make themselves generally useful. Most of these boys were the sons of chiefs. When they were not occupied with some errand, they would lounge about playing games with one another in the open space just by the King's hut.

Often when Mackay came to speak with the King, he had to wait in this place before he could have audience of M'tesa. He would bring with him large sheets of paper on which he had printed in his workshop the alphabet and some sentences. The printing was actually done with the little hand-press that Mackay had used in his attic when he was a boy in his old home in Rhynie. He had taken it with him all the way to Uganda, and now was setting up letters and sentences in a language which had never been printed before.

The Baganda boys who had gathered round the White-Man-of-Work with wondering eyes, as he with his "magic" printed the sheets of paper, now crowded about him as he unrolled one of these white sheets with the curious black smudges on them. Mackay made the noise that we call A and then B, and pointed to these curious-shaped objects which we call the letters of the alphabet. Then he got them to make the noise and point to the letter that represented that sound. At last the keenest of the boys really could repeat the alphabet right through and begin to read whole words from another sheet--Baganda words--so that at length they could read whole sentences.

Two of these pioneer boys became very good scholars. One named Mukasa became a Christian and was baptised with the name Samweli (Samuel);

another called Kakumba was baptised Yusufu (Joseph). A third boy had been captured from a tribe in the north, and his skin was of a much lighter brown than that of the Baganda boys. This light-skinned captured slave was named Lugalama.

Each of these boys felt that it was a very proud day when at last he could actually read a whole sheet of printing from beginning to end in his own language--from "Our Father" down to "the Kingdom, the power and the glory, Amen."

One morning these page-boys leapt to their feet as they heard the familiar rattle of the drums that heralded the coming of King M'tesa. They bowed as he entered the hall and sat heavily on his stool, while his chiefs ranged themselves about him.

On a stool near the King sat Mackay, the White-Man-of-Work. His bronzed face was set in grim determination, for he knew that on that morning he had a difficult battle to fight.

Another loud battering of drum-heads filled the air. The entrance to the hut was darkened by a tall, swarthy Arab in long, flowing robes, followed by negro-bearers, who cast on the ground bales of cloth and guns. The Arab wore on his head a red fez, round which a coloured turban scarf was wound. He was a slave-trader from the coast, who had come from the East to M'tesa in Uganda to buy men and women and children to carry them away into slavery.

King M'tesa was himself not only a slave-trader but a slave-raider. He sent his fierce gangs of warriors out to raid a tribe away in the hills to the north. They would dash into a village, slay the men, and drag the boys and girls and women back to M'tesa as slaves. The bronze-skinned boy, Lugalama, was a young slave who had been captured on one of these bloodthirsty raids. And M'tesa, who often sent out his executioners to slay his own people by the hundred to please the dreaded and horrible god of small-pox, would also sell his people by the hundred to get guns for his soldiers.

The Arab slave-trader bowed to the earth before King M'tesa, who signalled to him to speak.

"I have come," said the Arab, pointing to the guns on the floor, "to bring you these things in exchange for some men and women and children. See, I offer you guns and percussion caps and cloth." And he spread out lengths of the red cloth, and held out one of the guns with its gleaming barrel.

King M'tesa's eyes lighted up with desire as he saw the muskets and the ammunition. These, he thought, are the things that will make me powerful against my enemies.

"I will give you," the Arab slave-trader went on, "one of these lengths of red cloth in exchange for one man to be sold to me as a slave; one of these guns for two men; and one hundred of these percussion caps for a woman as a slave."

Mackay looked into the cruel face of M'tesa, and he could see how the ambitious King longed for the guns. Should he risk the favour of the King by fighting the battle of a few slaves? Yet Mackay remembered as he sat there, how Livingstone's great fight against the slave-traders had made him, as a student, vow that he too would go out and fight slavery in Africa. The memory nerved him for the fight he was now to make.

Mackay turned to M'tesa and said words like these:[55]

"O King M'tesa, you are set as father over all your multitude of people. They are your children. It is they who make you a great King.

"Remember, O King, that the Sultan of Zanzibar himself has signed a decree that no slaves shall be taken in all these lands and sold to other lands down beyond the coast, whither this Arab would lead your children. Therefore if you sell slaves you break his law.

"Will you, then, sell your own people that they may be taken out of their homeland into a strange country? They will be chained to one another, beaten with whips, scourged and kicked, and many will be left at the wayside to die; till the peoples of the coast shall laugh at Uganda and say, 'That is how King M'tesa lets strangers treat his children!'"

We can imagine how the Arab turned and scowled fiercely at Mackay. His heart raged, and he would have given anything to plunge the dagger hidden in his robe into Mackay's heart. Who was this white man who dared to try to stop his trade? But Mackay went on.

"See," he said, pointing to the boys and the chiefs, "your children are wonderfully made. Their bones, which are linked together, are clothed with flesh; and from the heart in their breasts the blood that gives men life flows to and fro through their bodies, while the breath goes in and out of their lungs and makes them live. God the Father and Maker of all men alone can create such wonders. No men who ever lived could, if they worked all through their lives, make one thing so marvellous as one of these boys. Will you, then, sell one of these miracles, one of your children, for a bit of red rag which any man can make in a day?"

All eyes turned to King M'tesa to learn what he would say.

The King with a wave of his hand dismissed the scowling Arab, while he took counsel with his chiefs, and came to this decision:

"My people shall no more be made slaves."

A decree was written out and King M'tesa put his hand to it. The crestfallen Arab and his men gathered up their guns and cloths, marched down the hill to buy ivory instead of slaves for their bales of red cloth, and went out of the dominions of King M'tesa, across the Great Lake homeward.

Mackay had won the first battle against slavery. His heart was very glad. Yet he knew that, although he had scored a triumph in this fight with the slave-dealer, he had not won in his great campaign. The King was generally kind to Mackay, for he was proud to have so clever a white man in his country. But he could not make up his mind to become a Christian. M'tesa's heart had not really changed. His slave-raiding of other tribes might still go on. The horrible butcherings of his people to turn away the dreaded anger of the gods would continue. Mackay felt he must press on with his work. He was slowly opening a road through the jungle of cruelty and the marshes of dread of the gods that made the life of the Baganda people dark and dreadful.

All Uganda waited breathless one day as though the end of the world had come.

"King M'tesa is dead!" the cry went out through all the land.

The people waited in dread and on tiptoe of eagerness till the new king was selected by the chiefs from the sons of the dead ruler.

At last a great cheer went up from the Palace. "M'wanga has eaten Uganda!" they shouted.

By this the people meant that M'wanga, a young son of M'tesa--only eighteen years old--had been made King. He was, however, a boy with no power--the mere feeble tool of the Katikiro (the Prime Minister) and of Mujasi, the Captain of the King's own bodyguard of soldiers. Both of these great men of the kingdom fiercely hated Mackay, for they were jealous of his power over the old King. So they whispered into the young M'wanga's ears stories like this: "You know that men say that Uganda will be eaten up by an enemy from the lands of the rising sun. Mackay and the other white men are making ready to bring thousands of white soldiers into your land to 'eat it up' and to kill you."

So M'wanga began to refuse to speak to Mackay. Then, because the King was afraid to attack him, he began to lay plots against the boys.

One morning Mackay started out from his house with five or six boys and the crew of his boat to march down to the lake. Among the boys were young Lugalama--the fair-haired slave-boy, now a freed-slave and a servant to Mackay--and Kakumba, who had (you remember) been baptised Joseph. The King and the Katikiro had given Mackay permission to go down to the lake and sail across it to take letters to a place called Msalala from which the carriers would bear them down to the coast.

Down the hill the party walked, the crew carrying the baggage and the oars on their heads. Mackay and his colleague Ashe, who had come out from England to work with him, walked behind.

To their surprise there came running down the path behind them and past them a company of soldiers.

"Where are you going?" asked Mackay of one of the soldiers.

"Mujasi, the Captain of the Bodyguard," he replied, "has sent us to capture some of the King's wives who have run away."

Another and yet another body of soldiers rushed past them. Mackay became more and more suspicious that some foul plot was being brewed. He and his company had walked ten miles, and the lake was but two miles away, divided from them by a wood. Suddenly there leapt out from behind the trees of the wood hundreds of men headed by Mujasi himself.

They levelled their guns and spears at Mackay and his friends and yelled, "Go back! Go back!"

"We are the King's friends," replied Mackay, "and we have his leave to travel. How dare you insult us?"

And they pushed forward. But the soldiers rushed at them; snatched their walking-sticks from them and began to jostle them. Mackay and Ashe sat down by the side of the path. Mujasi came up to them.

"Where are you walking?" he asked.

"We are travelling to the port with the permission of King M'wanga and the Katikiro."

"You are a liar!" replied Mujasi.

Mujasi stood back and the soldiers rushed at the missionaries, dragged them to their feet and held the muzzles of their guns within a few inches of their chests. Mackay turned with his boys and marched back to the capital.

He and Ashe were allowed to go back to their own home on the side of the hill, but the five boys were marched to the King's headquarters and imprisoned. The Katikiro, when Mackay went to him, refused to listen at first. Then he declared that Mackay was always taking boys out of the country, and returning with armies of white men and hiding them with the intention of conquering Uganda.

The Katikiro waved them aside and the angry waiting mob rushed on the missionaries yelling, "Mine shall be his coat!" "Mine his trousers!" "No, mine!" shouted another, as the men scuffled with one another.

Mackay and Ashe at last got back to their home and knelt in prayer. Later on the same evening, they decided to attempt to win back the King and the Prime Minister and Mujasi by gifts, so that their imprisoned boys would be freed from danger.

Mackay spoke to his other boys, telling them to go and fly for their lives or they would be killed.

In the morning Mackay heard that three of the boys who had been captured on the previous day were not only bound as prisoners, but that Mujasi was threatening to burn them to death. The boys were named Seruwanga, Kakumba, and Lugalama. The eldest was fifteen, the youngest twelve.

The boys were led out with a mob of howling men and boys around them. Mujasi shouted to them: "Oh, you know Isa Masiya (Jesus Christ). You believe you will rise from the dead. I shall burn you, and you will see if this is so."

A hideous roar of laughter rose from the mob. The boys were led down the hill towards the edge of a marsh. Behind them was a plantation of banana trees. Some men who had carried bundles of firewood on their heads threw the wood into a heap; others laid hold of each of the boys and cut off their arms with hideous curved knives so that they should not struggle in the fire.

Seruwanga, the bravest, refused to utter a cry as he was cut to pieces, but Kakumba shouted to Mujasi, who was a Mohammedan, "You believe in Allah the Merciful. Be merciful!" But Mujasi had no mercy.

We are told that the men who were watching held their breath with awed amazement as they heard a boy's voice out of the flame and smoke singing,

"Daily, daily sing to Jesus, Sing, my soul, His praises due."

As the executioners came towards the youngest and feeblest, Lugalama, he cried, "Oh, do not cut off my arms. I will not struggle, I will not fight--only throw me into the fire."

But they did their ghastly work, and threw the mutilated boy on a wooden framework above the slow fire where his cries went up, till at last there was silence.

One other Christian stood by named Musali. Mujasi, with eyes bloodshot and inflamed with cruelty, came towards him and cried:

"Ah, you are here. I will burn you too and your household. You are a follower of Isa (Jesus)."

"Yes, I am," replied Musali, "and I am not ashamed of it."

It was a marvel of courage to say in the face of the executioner's fire and knife what Peter dared not say when the servant-maid in Jerusalem laughed at him. Perhaps the heroism of Musali awed even the cruel-hearted Mujasi. In any case he left Musali alone.

For a little time M'wanga ceased to persecute the Christians. But the wily Arabs whispered in his ear that the white men were still trying to "eat up" his country. M'wanga was filled with mingled anger and fear. Then his fury burst all bounds when Mujasi said to him: "There is a great white man coming from the rising sun. Behind him will come thousands of white soldiers."

"Send at once and kill him," cried the demented M'wanga.

A boy named Balikudembe, a Christian, heard the order and he could not contain himself, but broke out, "Oh, King M'wanga, why are you going to kill a white man? Your father did not do so."

But the soldiers went out, travelled east along the paths till they met the great Bishop Hannington being carried in a litter, stricken with fever. They took him prisoner, and, after some days, slew him as he stood defenceless before them. Hannington had been sent out to help Mackay and his fellow-

Christians.

Then the King fell ill. He believed that the boy Balikudembe, who had warned him not to kill the Bishop, had bewitched him. So M'wanga's soldiers went and caught the lad and led him down to a place where they lit a fire, and placing the boy over it, burned him slowly to death.

All through this time Mackay alone had not been really seriously threatened, for his work and what he was made the King and the Katikiro and even Mujasi afraid to do him to death.

Then there came a tremendous thunderstorm. A flash of lightning smote the King's house and it flamed up and burned to ashes. Then King M'wanga seemed to go mad. He threatened to slay Mackay himself.

"Take, seize, burn the Christians," he cried. And his executioners and their minions rushed out, captured forty-six men and boys, slashed their arms from their bodies with their cruel curved knives so that they could not struggle, and then placed them over the ghastly flames which slowly wrung the lives from their tortured bodies. Yet the numbers of the Christians seemed to grow with persecution.

The King himself beat one boy, Apolo Kagwa, with a stick and smote him on the head, then knocked him down, kicked and stamped upon him. Then the King burned all his books, crying, "Never read again."

The other men and boys who had become Christians were now scattered over the land in fear of their lives. Mackay, however, come what may, determined to hold on. He set his little printing press to work and printed off a letter which he sent to the scattered Christians. In Mackay's letter was written these words, "In days of old Christians were hated, were hunted, were driven out and were persecuted for Jesus' sake, and thus it is to-day. Our beloved brothers, do not deny our Lord Jesus!"

At last M'wanga's mad cruelties grew so frightful that all his people rose in rebellion and drove him from the throne, so that he had to wander an outcast by the lake-side. Mackay at that time was working by the lake, and he offered to shelter the deposed King who had only a short time before threatened his life.

* * * * *

Two years passed; and Mackay, on the lake-side, was building a new boat in which he hoped to sail to other villages to teach the people. Then a fever struck him. He lay lingering for some days. Then he died--aged only forty-one.

If Mackay, instead of becoming a missionary, had entered the engineering profession he might have become a great engineer. When he was a missionary in Africa, the British East Africa Company offered him a good position. He refused it. General Gordon offered him a high position in his army in Egypt. He refused it.

He held on when his friends and the Church Missionary Society called him home. This is what he said to them, "What is this you write--'Come home'? Surely now, in our terrible dearth of workers, it is not the time for anyone to desert his post. Send us only our first twenty men, and I may be tempted to come to help you to find the second twenty."

He died when quite young; homeless, after a life in constant danger from fever and from a half-mad tyrant king--his Christian disciples having been burned.

Was it worth while?

To-day the Prime Minister of Uganda is Apolo Kagwa, who as a boy was kicked and beaten and stamped upon by King M'wanga for being a Christian; and the King of Uganda, Daudi, M'wanga's son, is a Christian. At the capital there stands a fine cathedral in which brown Baganda clergy lead the prayers of the Christian people. On the place where the boys were burned to death there stands a Cross, put there by 70,000 Baganda Christians in memory of the young martyrs.

Was their martyrdom worth while?

To-day all the slave raiding has ceased for ever; innocent people are not slaughtered to appease the gods; the burning of boys alive has ceased.

Mackay began the work. He made the first rough road and as he made it he wrote: "This will certainly yet be a highway for the King Himself; and all that pass this way will come to know His name."

"And a highway shall be there and a way; and it shall be a way of holiness."

But the Way is not finished. And the last words that Mackay wrote were: "Here is a sphere for your energies. Bring with you your highest education and your greatest talents, and you will find scope for the exercise of them all."

FOOTNOTES:

[Footnote 55: There is no record of the precise words, but Mackay gives the argument in a letter home.]

CHAPTER XXI

THE BLACK APOSTLE OF THE LONELY LAKE

Shomolekae

In the garden in Africa where, you remember, David Livingstone plighted troth with Mary Moffat, as they stood under an almond tree, there lived years ago a chocolate-skinned, curly-haired boy. His name was Shomolekae.[56]

His work was to go among the fruit trees, when the peaches and apricots were growing and to shout and make a noise to scare away the birds. If he had not done this they would have eaten up all the fruit. This boy was born in Africa over seventy-five years ago, when Victoria was a young queen.

In the same garden was a grown-up gardener, also an African, with a dark face and crisp, curly hair. The grown-up gardener one day stole some of the fruit off the trees, and he went to the little boy, Shomolekae, and offered him some apricots.

Now, Shomolekae had learned to love the missionary, Mr. Mackenzie, who had come to live in the house at Kuruman. He knew that it was very wrong of the gardener to steal the fruit and throw the blame on the birds. So he said that he would not touch the fruit. He went to an old black friend of his named Paul and said to him:

"The gardener has stolen the apples and plums and has asked me to eat them. He has robbed Mr. Mackenzie. I do not know what to do."

And old Paul went and told John Mackenzie, who took notice of the boy Shomolekae and learned to trust him.

Many months passed by; and two years later John Mackenzie was going to a place further north in Africa than Kuruman. The name of this town was Shoshong, where Mackenzie would live and teach the people about Jesus Christ. So he went to the father of Shomolekae, whose name was Sebolai.

"Sebolai," said John Mackenzie, "I want to take your son, Shomolekae, with me to Shoshong."

Sebolai replied: "I am willing that my son should come to live with you, but one thing I desire. It is that he should be taught his reading and to know the stories in the Bible and such things."

To this John Mackenzie quickly agreed, for he too desired that the boy should read.

So the sixteen oxen were yoked to the big wagon, and amid much shouting and cracking of whips and lowing of oxen and creaking of wagon-joints, John Mackenzie, Shomolekae, and the others, started from Kuruman northward to Shoshong.

Now, at Shoshong the chief was Sekhome, who, you remember, in our last story, was father to Khama. So when they were at Shoshong, Shomolekae, the young man who was cook, and Khama, the young man who was the son of the chief, worshipped in the same little church together. It was not such a church as you go to in our country--but just a little place made of mud bricks that had been dried in the sun. There were holes instead of windows, and there was no door in the open doorway; and on the top of the little building was a roof of rough, reedy grass.

These were the days that you heard of in the last story, when Khama, seeing his tribe attacked by the fierce Lobengula, rode out on horseback at the head of his regiment of cavalry and fought them and beat them, and drove away Lobengula with a bullet in his neck.

For two years Shomolekae, learning to read better every day, and serving John Mackenzie faithfully in his house, lived at Shoshong.

Sometimes Shomolekae took long journeys with wagon and oxen, and at the end of two years he went with Mackenzie a great way in order to buy windows, doors, hinges, nails, corrugated iron, and timber with which to build a better church at Shoshong.

When Shomolekae came back again with the wagons loaded up there was great excitement in the tribe. Hammers and saws, screw-drivers and chisels were busy day after day, and the missionary and his helpers laid the bricks one upon another until there rose up a strong church with windows and a door--a place in which the people went to worship God the Father of our Lord Jesus Christ.

Again Shomolekae went away by wagon, and this time he travelled away by the edge of the desert southward until at last he reached the garden at Kuruman where as a boy he used to frighten the birds from the fruit trees. He was now a very clever man at driving wagons and oxen.

This, as you know, is not so easy as driving a wagon with two horses is in Britain. For there were as many as sixteen and even eighteen oxen harnessed two by two to the long iron chains in front of the wagon.

There were no roads, only rough tracks, and the wagon would drag through the deep sand, or bump over great boulders of rock, or sink into wet places by the river. But at such times one of the natives always led the two front oxen through the river with a long thong that was fastened to their horns.

So, in order to drive a wagon well, Shomolekae needed to be able to manage sixteen oxen all at once, and keep them walking in a straight line. He needed to know which were the bad-tempered ones and which were the good, and which pulled best in one part of the span and which in another; and how to keep them all pulling together and not lunging at one another with their horns.

Shomolekae also had to be so bold and daring that, if lions came to eat the oxen at night, he could go with the gun and either frighten them away or actually shoot them.

So you see Shomolekae was very clever, and was full of good courage.

While he was living at Kuruman a man came to him one day and said:

"John Mackenzie is alone at Shoshong, and there is no one who can drive his wagon well for him."

The man who told him this was, as it happened, going by wagon to Shoshong, where John Mackenzie lived.

"Let me go with you," said Shomolekae.

So he got up into the wagon, and away they went day after day northward on the same journey that Shomolekae had taken when he was a boy.

So Shomolekae served Mackenzie for years as wagon driver at Shoshong.

At last the time came when Mackenzie himself left the tribe at Shoshong--left Khama and all his people--and travelled southward to build at Kuruman a kind of small school where he could train young black men to be missionaries to their own people. And Shomolekae himself went to Kuruman with Mackenzie. He set to work with his own hands, and he helped to make and lay bricks, to put in the doors and windows, and to place the roof on the walls, until at last the little school was built.

And when it was actually built Shomolekae himself went to be a student there, and Mackenzie began to train him to be a preacher and a teacher to his own people.

For three years Shomolekae worked hard in the college, learning more and more about Jesus Christ, preparing himself to go among his own people to tell them about Him.

At last the time came when he was ready to go; and he started out, and travelled long, long miles through sandy places, and then by a river, until at last he reached a town of little thatched huts called Pitsani, which means "The Town of the Little Hyena."

In that town he gathered the men and women and the boys and girls together and taught them the things that he knew.

While Shomolekae was at Pitsani there came into that part of Africa a new missionary, whose name was Mr. Wookey.

It was decided that Mr. Wookey should go a long, long journey and settle down by the shores of Lake Ngami, which, you remember, David Livingstone had discovered long years before.

Shomolekae wished to go out with Mr. Wookey into this country and to help. So he took the wagon and yoked the oxen to it, loaded it up with food and all the things needed for cooking as they travelled along, and drove the oxen dragging the wagon over many hundreds of miles of country in which leopards barked and lions roared, until at last they came to the land near Lake Ngami.

When they came into this land, and found a place in which to settle down, clever Shomolekae mixed earth into mud just as boys and girls do in order to make mud-pies, but he made the mud into the shape of bricks, and then placed the bricks of mud out into the sun to dry.

The sunshine was very, very hot indeed--so hot that the bricks became hard and dry and strong. Day after day Shomolekae worked until he had made a big heap of bricks. With these he built a little house for Mr. Wookey to live in. But these sun-dried bricks soon spoil if they get wet, so he had to build a verandah to keep the rain from the walls.

When the house was built and Mr. Wookey was settled in it, they travelled still further up the river to learn what people were living there.

After a while it was decided that Shomolekae should go and live in a small village by the river, and there again begin his work of telling the men and women of Jesus Christ, and teaching the boys and girls to read.

In his satchel, which was made of odd bits of calico print of different patterns, Shomolekae had a hymn-book with music. The hymn-book was written in the language of the people--the Sechuana language--and Shomolekae taught them from the book to sing hymns. The music was the sol-fa notation.

This is one of the hymns:

1. "Yesu oa me oa nthata, Leha ke le mo dibin; A re yalo mo kwalon, A re yalo mo pedun.

E, Yesu oa me, E, Yesu oa me, E, Yesu oa me, Oa me, mo loraton.

2. "Yesu oa me oa nthata, O ntehetse molato; O mpusitse timelon, O ntlhapisa mo pedun.

"E, Yesu oa me," etc.

This is what these words mean in English. I expect you know them very well.

1. "Jesus loves me, this I know, For the Bible tells me so; Little ones to Him belong, They are weak, but He is strong.

"Yes, Jesus loves me, Yes, Jesus loves me, Yes, Jesus loves me-- The Bible tells me so.

2. "Jesus loves me, He who died Heaven's gate to open wide; He will wash away my sin, Let His little child come in.

"Yes, Jesus loves me," etc.

But, you see, the missionary had to alter the words sometimes so as to make the Sechuana lines come right for the music; and the second verse really means:

"My Jesus loves me; He has paid my debt; He has brought me back from where I strayed; He has washed my heart.

Yes, my Jesus, Yes, my Jesus. Yes, my Jesus. Mine in love."

They would learn the words off by heart because there was only the one hymn-book, and they would sing them together, Shomolekae's voice leading.

They learned them so well that sometimes when the mothers were out hoeing in the fields, or the little boys were paddling in their canoes and fishing in the marshy waters, you would hear them singing the hymns that they learned in Shomolekae's little school hut.

Then on Sunday they would have Sunday-school, and when that was over Shomolekae would gather the chocolate-faced men and women and boys and girls together--all who would come--and he would teach them to kneel down and pray to the one God, Who is our Father, and they would sing the hymns that they had learned, and then he would speak to them a simple little address, telling them of the Lord Jesus.

But Shomolekae desired always to go further and further, even though it was dangerous and difficult. So he got a canoe and launched it in the river by the village and paddled further and further up the stream, under the overhanging trees, and sometimes across the deep pools in which the big and fierce hippopotami and crocodiles lived.

He paddled up the River Okanvango, though many times he was in danger of his life. The river was not like rivers in our own country, deep and with strong banks; it was often filled all over with reeds, and as shallow as a swamp, and poor Shomolekae had to push his way with difficulty through these reeds. Always at night the poisonous mosquitoes came buzzing and humming around him. The evil-tempered hippopotamus would suddenly come up from the bottom of the river with his wicked beady eyes, and great cavernous mouth, with its enormous teeth, yawning at Shomolekae as though he quite meant to swallow him whole.

On the banks at night the lions would roar, and then the hyenas would howl; but Shomolekae's brave heart held on, and he pushed on up the river to preach and teach the people in the villages near the river.

So through many years, with high courage and simple faith, Shomolekae worked.

A good many boys and girls in England before they are ten years old own many more books than Shomolekae ever had and have read more than he. They also have better homes than he, for he pushed on from one mud hut to another along the rivers and lakes, and all the possessions that he had in the world could be put into the bottom of his canoe.

But our Heavenly Father, Who loves you and me, went with him every step of the way. When Shomolekae taught the boys and girls to sing hymns in praise of Jesus, even in a little mud hut, He was there, just as He is in the most beautiful church when we worship Him. Now God has taken Shomolekae across the last river to be with Himself.

Shomolekae was a negro with dark skin and curly hair. We are white children with fair faces and light hair. But God is his Father as well as ours and loves us all alike and wishes to gather us together round Him--loving Him and one another.

FOOTNOTES:

[Footnote 56: Pronounce Shoh-moh-leh-kei.]

CHAPTER XXII

THE WOMAN WHO CONQUERED CANNIBALS

Mary Slessor (Dates, b. 1848, d. 1915)

I. THE MILL-GIRL

The Calabar Girls at the Station As the train from the south slowed down in Waverley Station, Edinburgh, one day in 1898, a black face, with eyes wide open with wonder, appeared at the window. The carriage door opened and a little African girl was handed down onto the platform.

The people on the station stopped to glance at the strange negro face. But as a second African girl a little older than the first stepped from the carriage to the platform, and a third, and then a fourth black girl appeared, the cabmen and porters stood staring in amused curiosity.

Who was that strange woman (they asked one another), short and slight, with a face like yellow parchment and with short, straight brown hair, who smiled as she gathered the little tribe of African girls round her on the railway platform?

The telegraph boys and the news-boys gazed at her in astonishment. But they would have been transfixed with amazement if they had known a tenth of the wonder of the story of that heroic woman who, just as simply as she stood there on the Waverley platform, had mastered cannibals, conquered wild drunken chiefs brandishing loaded muskets, had faced hunger and thirst under the flaming heat and burning fevers of Africa, and walked unscathed by night through forests haunted by ferocious leopards, to triumph over regiments of frenzied savages drawn up for battle, had rescued from death hundreds of baby twins thrown out to be eaten by ants--and had now brought home to Scotland from West Africa four of these her rescued children.

Still more would those Scottish boys at Waverley Station have wondered, as they gazed on the little woman and her group of black children, if they had known that the woman who had done these things, Mary Slessor, had been a Scottish factory girl, who had toiled at her weaving machine from six in the morning till six at night amid the whirr of the belts, the flash of the shuttles, the rattle of the looms, and the roar of the great machines.

Born in Aberdeen, December 2, 1848, Mary Slessor was the daughter of a Scottish shoemaker. Her mother was a gentle and sweet-faced woman. After her father's death Mary was the mainstay of the home. Working in a weaving shed in Dundee (whither the family moved when Mary was eleven) she educated herself while at her machine.

The Call to Africa Like Livingstone, she taught herself with her book propped up on the machine at which she worked. She read his travels and heard the stories of his fight against slavery for Africa, till he became her hero.

One day the news flashed round the world: "Livingstone is dead. His heart is buried in Central Africa." Mary had thrilled as she read the story of his heroic and lonely life. Now he had fallen. She heard in her heart the words that he had spoken:

"I go to Africa to try to make an open door....; do you carry out the work which I have begun. I LEAVE IT WITH YOU."

As Mary sat, tired with her week's work, in her pew in the church on Sunday, and thought of Livingstone's call to Africa, she saw visions of far-off places of which she heard from the pulpit and read in her magazines--visions of a steaming river on the West Coast of Africa where the alligators slid from the mud banks into the water; visions of the barracoons on the shore in which the captured negroes were penned as they waited for the slave-ships; pictures of villages where trembling prisoners dipped their hands in boiling oil to test their guilt, and wives were strangled to go with their dead chief into the spirit-land; visions of the fierce chiefs who could order a score of men to be beheaded for a cannibal feast and then sell a hundred more to be hounded away into the outer darkness of slavery--the Calabar where the missionaries of her church were fighting the black darkness of the most savage people of the world.

Mary Slessor made up her mind to go out and give her whole life to Africa. So she offered herself, a timorous girl who could not cross a field with a cow in it, as a missionary for cannibal Calabar, in West Africa.

For twelve years she worked at the centre of the mission in Calabar and then flung herself into pioneer work among the terrible tribe of Okoyong. No one had ever been able to influence them. They defied British administration. For fifteen years she strove there, and won a power over the ferocious Okoyong savages such as no one has ever wielded. "I'm a wee, wee wifie," she said, "no very bookit, but I grip on well none the less."

To-day over two thousand square miles of forest and rivers, the dark savages, as they squat at night in the forest around their palaver-fires, tell one another stories of the Great-White-Ma-Who-Lived-Alone, and the stories they tell are like these.

II. THE HEALING OF THE CHIEF

Through the Forest in the Rain A strange quiet lay over all the village by the river. For the chief lay ill in his hut. The Calabar people were waiting on the tip-toe of suspense. For if the chief died many of them would be slain to go with him into the spirit-world--his wives and some of his soldiers and slaves.

Suddenly a strange African woman, who had come over from another village, entered the chief's harem. She spoke to the wives of the chief, saying, "There lives away through the forest at Ekenge a white Ma who can cast out by her magic the demons who are killing your chief. My son's child was dying, but the white Ma[57] saved her and she is well to-day. Many other wonders has she done by the power of her juju. Let your chief send for her and he will not die."

There was silence and then eager chattering, for the women knew that their very lives depended on the chief getting well. If he died, they would be killed.

They sent in word to the chief about the strange white Ma.

"Let her be sent for," he ordered. "Send a bottle and four rods (value about a shilling) and messengers to ask her to come."

All through the day the messengers hurried over stream and hill, through village after village and along the forest paths till at last, after eight hours' journey, they came to the village of Ekenge. Going to the courtyard of the chief they told him the story of their sick chief, and their desire that the white Ma who lived in his village should come and heal him.

"She will say for herself what she will do," said the chief.

So he sent a messenger to Mary Slessor. She soon came over from her little house to learn what was needed of her.

The story of the sick chief was again told.

"What is the matter with your chief?" asked Mary Slessor. Blank faces and nodding heads showed that they knew nothing at all.

"I must go to him," she declared. She knew that the way was full of perils, and that she might be killed by warriors and wild beasts; but she knew too that, if she did not go and if the chief died, hundreds of lives might be sacrificed.

Chief Edem said, "There are warriors out in the woods and you will be killed. You must not go."

Ma Eme, a tall fat African widow of Ekenge village, who loved Mary Slessor, said, "No, you must not go. The streams are deep; the rains are come. You could never get there."

But Mary Slessor said, "I must go."

"Then I will send women with you to look after you, and men to protect you," said Chief Edem.

Mary Slessor went back to her house to prepare to start on her long dangerous journey in the morning. She could not sleep for wondering whether she was indeed right to risk her life and all her work on the off-chance of saving this distant sick chief. She knelt down and asked God to guide her. Then she felt in her heart that she must go.

In the morning at dawn a guard of Ekenge women came to her door.

"The men will join us outside the village," they said.

The skies were grey. The rain was falling as they started. When the village lay behind them the rain began to pour in sheets. It came down as only an African rain can, unceasing torrents of pitiless deluge. Soon Mary Slessor's soaked boots became impossible to walk in. She took them off and threw them into the bush; then her stockings went, and she ploughed on in the mud in her bare feet.

They had walked for three hours when, as the weather began to clear, Mary Slessor came out into a market-place for neighbouring villages. The hundreds of Africans who were bartering in the market-place turned and stared at the strange white woman who swiftly passed through their midst and disappeared into the bush beyond.

So she pressed on for hour after hour, her head throbbing with fever, her dauntless spirit driving her trembling, timid body onward till at last, when she had been walking almost ceaselessly for over eight hours, she tottered into the village of the sick chief.

The Healing Hand.

Mary Slessor, aching from head to foot with fever and overwhelming weariness, did not lie down even for a moment's rest, but walked straight to the chief who lay senseless on his mat on the mud floor. Having examined him she took from her little medicine chest a drug and gave a dose to the chief. But she could see at once that more of this medicine was needed than she had with her. She knew that, away on the other side of the river, some hours distant, another missionary was working.

"You must go across the river to Ikorofiong for more medicine."

"No, no!" they said, "we dare not go. They will slay any man who goes there."

She was in despair. Then someone said, "There is a man of that country living in his canoe on the river. Perhaps he would go?"

They ran down to the river and found him. After much persuading he at last went, and returned next day with the medicine.

The chief, whom the women had believed to be almost dead, gradually recovered consciousness, then sat up and took food. At last he was quite well. All the village laughed and sang for joy. There would be no slaying. They gathered round Mary Slessor in grateful wonder at her magic powers. She told them that she had come to them because she worshipped the Great Physician Jesus Christ, the Son of the Father--God who made all things. Then she gathered them together in the morning and evening, and led them as with bowed heads they all thanked God for the healing of the chief.

III. VALIANT IN FIGHT

Years passed by and Mary Slessor's name was known in all the villages for many miles. She was, to them, the white Ma who was brave and wise and kind. She was mad, they thought, because she was always rescuing the twin babies whom the Calabar people throw out to die and the mothers of twins whom they often kill. But in some strange way they felt that her wisdom, her skill in healing men, and her courage, which was more heroic than that of their bravest warriors, came from the Spirit who made all things. She would wrench guns from the hands of drunken savage men who were three times as strong as she was. At last she used to sit with their chief as judge of quarrels, and many times in palavers between villages she stopped the people from going to war.

Through the Forest Perilous One day a secret message came to her that, in some villages far away, a man of one village had wounded the chief in another village and that all the warriors were arming and holding councils of war.

"I must go and stop it," said Mary Slessor.

"You cannot," said her friends at Ekenge, "the steamer is coming to take you home to Britain because you are so ill. You will miss the boat. You are too ill to walk. The wild beasts in the woods will kill you. The savage warriors are out, and will kill you in the dark--not knowing who you are."

"But I must go," she answered.

The chief insisted that she must have two armed men with lanterns with her, and that she must get the chief of a neighbouring village to send out his drummer with her so that people might know--as they heard the drum--that a protected person was travelling who must not be harmed.

It was night, and Mary Slessor with her two companions marched out into the darkness, the lanterns throwing up strange shadows that looked like fierce men in the darkness. Through the night they walked till at midnight they reached the village where they were to ask for the drum.

The chief was surly.

"You are going to a warlike people," he said. "They will not listen to what a woman says. You had better go back. I will not protect you."

Mary Slessor was on her mettle.

"When you think of the woman's power," she said to the chief, "you forget the power of the woman's God. I shall go on."

And to the amazement of the savages in the villages she went on into the darkness. Surely she must be mad. She defied their chief who had the power to kill her. She had walked on into a forest where ferocious leopards abounded ready to spring out upon her, and where men were drinking themselves into a fury of war. And for what? To try with a woman's tongue to stop the fiery chiefs and the savages of a distant warlike tribe from fighting. Surely she was mad.

Facing the Warriors She pressed on through the darkness. Then she saw the dim outlines of huts. Mary Slessor had reached the first town in the war area. She found the hut where an old Calabar woman lived who knew the white Ma.

"Who is there?" came a whisper from within.

But even as she replied there was a swift patter of bare feet. Out of the darkness leapt a score of armed warriors. They were all round her. From all parts dark shadows sprang forward till scores of men with their chiefs were jostling, chattering and threatening.

"What have you come for?" they asked.

"I have heard that you are going to war. I have come to ask you not to fight," she replied.

The chiefs hurriedly talked together, then they came to her and said--

"The white Ma is welcome. She shall hear all that we have to say before we fight. All the same we shall fight. For here you see are men wounded. We must wipe out the disgrace that is put upon us. Now she must rest. Women, you take care of the white Ma. We will call her at cock-crow when we start."

This meant an hour's sleep. Mary Slessor lay down in a hut. It seemed as though her eyes were hardly shut before she was wakened again. She stood, tottering with tiredness, when she heard the cry--

"Run, Ma, run!"

The warriors were off down the hill away to the fight. She ran, but they were quickly out of sight on the way to the attack. Was all her trouble in vain? She pressed on weak and breathless, but determined. She heard wild yells and the roll of the war drum. The warriors she had followed were feverishly making ready to fight, a hundred yards distant from the enemy's village.

She went up to them and spoke sternly.

"Behave like men," she said, "not like fools. Do not yell and shout. Hold your peace. I am going into the village there."

She pointed to the enemy. Then she walked forward. Ahead of her stood the enemy in unbroken ranks of dark warriors. They stood like a solid wall. She hailed them as she walked forward.

There was an ominous silence. She laughed.

"How perfect your manners are!" she exclaimed. She was about to walk forward and force them to make way for her when an old chief stepped out toward her and, to her amazement, knelt down at her feet.

"Ma," he said, "we thank you for coming to us. We own that we wounded the chief over there. It was only one of our men who did it. It was not the act of all our town. We ask you that you will speak with our enemy to bring them to peace with us."

The Healed Chief She looked into the face of the chief. Then she saw to her joy that this was the very chief whom she had toiled through the rain to heal long ago. Because of what she had done then, he was now at her feet asking her to make peace. Should she run back and tell the warriors, who a hundred yards away were spoiling for a fight? That was her first joyful thought. Then she saw that she must first make her authority stronger over the whole band of warriors.

"Stay where you are," she said. "Some of you find a place where I can sit in comfort; and bring me food. I will not starve while men fight. Choose two or three men to speak well for you, and we will have two men from your enemies."

These grim warriors, so sullen and threatening a few moments ago, obeyed her every word. At length two chiefs came from the other side and stood on one side of her, while the two chiefs chosen in the village came and threw down their arms and knelt at their feet.

"Your chief," they said, "was wounded by a drunken youth. Do not let us shed blood through all our villages because of what he did. If you will cease from war with us, we will pay to you any fine that the white Ma shall say."

She, too, pressed them to stop their fighting. Word went back to the warriors on both sides, who became wildly excited. Some agreed, others stormed and raged till they were in a frenzy. Would they fight even over her body? Furious warriors came moving up from both sides. But by arguing and appealing at last she persuaded the warlike tribe to accept a fine.

The Promise of Peace The town whose drunken youth had wounded the enemy chief at once paid a part of the fine. They used no money. So the fine was paid in casks and bottles of trade gin. Mary Slessor trembled. For as the boxes of gin bottles were brought forward the warriors pranced with excitement and made ready to get drunk. She knew that this would make them fight after all. What could she do? The roar of voices rose. She could not make her own voice heard. A daring idea flashed into her mind. According to the law of these Egbo people, clothes thrown over anything give it the protection of your body. She snatched off her skirt and all the clothing she could spare and spread them over the gin. She seized the one glass that the tribe had, and doled out one portion only to each chief to test whether the bottles indeed contained spirit. At last they grew quieter and she spoke to them.

"I am going," she said, "across the Great Waters to my home, and I shall be away many moons. Promise me here, on both sides, that you will not go to war with one another while I am away."

"We promise," they said. They gathered around her and she told them the story of Jesus Christ in whose name she had come to them.

"Now," she said, "go to your rest and fight no more." And the tribes kept their promise to her,--so that when she returned they could say, "It is peace."

* * * * *

For nearly forty years she worked on in Calabar, stricken scores of times with fever. She rescued her hundreds of twin babies thrown out to die in the forest, stopped wars and ordeal by poison, made peace, healed the sick.

At last, too weak to walk, she was wheeled through the forests and along the valleys by some of her "twins" now grown to strong children, and died there--the conquering Queen of Calabar, who ruled in the hearts of even the fiercest cannibals through the power of the Faith, by which out of weakness she was made strong.

FOOTNOTES:

[Footnote 57: The African uses the word "Ma" as mother, (_a_) to name a woman after her eldest son, _e.g._ Mrs. Livingstone was called Ma-Robert; and (_b_) as in this case, for a woman whom they respect.]

Book Four: HEROINES AND HEROES OF PLATEAU AND DESERT

CHAPTER XXIII

SONS OF THE DESERT

Abdallah and Sabat (Time of Incidents, about 1800-1810)

Two Arab Wanderers One day, more than a hundred years ago, two young Arabs, Abdallah and Sabat, rode on their camels toward a city that was hidden among the tawny hills standing upon the skyline.

The sun was beginning to drop toward the edge of the desert away in the direction of the Red Sea. The shadows of the long swinging legs of the camels wavered in grotesque lines on the sand. There was a look of excited expectation in the eyes of the young Arabs; for, by sunset, their feet would walk the city of their dreams.

They were bound for Mecca, the birthplace of Mohammed, the Holy City toward which every man of the Mohammedan world turns five times a day as he cries, "There is no God but Allah, and Mohammed is the prophet of Allah." To have worshipped in Mecca before the sacred Kaaba and to have kissed the black stone in its wall--this was to make Paradise certain for them both. Having done that pilgrimage these two Arabs, Sabat and Abdallah, would be able to take the proud title of "Haji" which would proclaim to every man that they had been to Mecca--the Holy of Holies.

So they pressed on by the valley between the hills till they saw before them the roofs and the minarets of Mecca itself. As darkness rushed across the desert and the stars came out, the tired camels knelt in the courtyard of the Khan,[58] and Sabat and Abdallah alighted and stretched their cramped legs, and took their sleep.

These young men, Sabat and Abdallah, the sons of notable Arab chiefs, had struck up a great friendship. Now, each in company with his chum, they were together at the end of the greatest journey that an Arab can take.

As the first faint flush of pink touched the mountain beyond Mecca, the cry came from the minaret: "Come to prayer. Prayer is better than sleep. There is no God but Allah."

Sabat and Abdallah were already up and out, and that day they said the Mohammedan prayer before the Kaaba itself with other pilgrims who had come from many lands--from Egypt and Abyssinia, from Constantinople and Damascus, Baghdad and Bokhara, from the defiles of the Khyber Pass, from the streets of Delhi and the harbour of Zanzibar.

We do not know what Abdallah looked like. He was probably like most young Arab chieftains, a tall, sinewy man--brown-faced, dark-eyed, with hair and a short-cropped beard that were between brown and black.

His friend Sabat was, however, so striking that even in that great crowd of many pilgrims people would turn to look at him. They would turn round, for one reason, because of Sabat's voice. Even when he was just talking to his friend his voice sounded like a roar; when he got excited and in a passion (as he very often did) it rolled like thunder and was louder than most men's shouting. As he spoke his large white teeth gleamed in his wide mouth. His brown face and black arched eyebrows were a dark setting for round eyes that flashed as he spoke. His black beard flowed over his tawny throat and neck. Gold earrings swung with his agitation and a gold chain gleamed round his neck. He wore a bright silk jacket with long sleeves, and long, loose-flowing trousers and richly embroidered shoes with turned-up toes. From a girdle round his waist hung a dagger whose handle and hilt flashed with jewels.

Abdallah and Sabat were better educated than most Arabs, for they could both read. But they were not men who could stay in one place and read and think in quiet. When they had finished their worship at Mecca, they determined to ride far away across the deserts eastward, even to Kabul in the mountains of Afghanistan. So they rode, first northward up the great camel-route toward Damascus, and then eastward. In spite of robbers and hungry jackals, through mountain gorges, over streams, across the Syrian desert from oasis to oasis, and then across the Euphrates and the Tigris they went, till they had climbed rung by rung the mountain ranges that hold up the great plateau of Persia.

At last they broke in upon the rocky valleys of Afghanistan and came to the gateway of India--to Kabul. They presented themselves to Zeman Shah, the ruler of Afghanistan, and he was so taken with Abdallah's capacity that he asked him to be one of his officers in the court. So Abdallah stayed in Kabul. But the restless, fiery Sabat turned the face of his camel westward and rode back into Persia to the lovely city of Bokhara.

Abdallah the Daring In Kabul there was an Armenian whose name we do not know: but he owned a book printed in Arabic, a book that Abdallah could read. The Armenian lent it to him. There were hardly any books in Arabic, so Abdallah took this book and read it eagerly. As he read, he thought that he had never in all his life heard of such wonderful things, and he could feel in his very bones that they were true. He read four short true stories in this book: they were what we call the Gospels according to Matthew, Mark, Luke and John. As he read, Abdallah saw in the stories Someone who was infinitely greater than Mohammed--One who was so strong and gentle that He was always helping children and women and people who were ill; so good that He always lived the very life that God willed; and so brave that He died rather than give in to evil men--our Lord Jesus Christ.

"I worship Him," said Abdallah in his heart. Then he did a very daring thing. He knew that if he turned Christian it would be the duty of Mohammedans to kill him. Why not keep quiet and say nothing about his change of heart? But he could not. He decided that he must come out in the open and confess the new Captain of his life. He was baptized a Christian.

The Moslems were furious. To save his life Abdallah fled on his camel westward to Bokhara. But the news that he had become a Christian flew even faster than he himself rode. As he went along the streets of Bokhara he saw his friend Sabat coming toward him. As a friend, Sabat desired to save Abdallah; but as a Moslem, the cruel law of Mohammed said that he must have him put to death. And Sabat was a fiery, hot-tempered Moslem.

"I had no pity," Sabat told his friends afterward. "I delivered him up to Morad Shah, the King."

So Abdallah was bound and carried before the Moslem judges. His friend Sabat stood by watching, just as Saul had stood watching them stone Stephen nearly eighteen centuries earlier.

"You shall be given your life and be set free," they said, "if you will spit upon the Cross and renounce Christ and say, 'There is no God but Allah.'"

"I refuse," said Abdallah.

A sword was brought forward and unsheathed. Abdallah's arm was stretched out: the sword was lifted--it flashed--and Abdallah's hand, cut clean off, fell on the ground, while the blood spurted from his arm.

"Your life will still be given you if you renounce Christ and proclaim Allah and Mohammed as His prophet."

This is how Sabat himself described what happened next. "Abdallah made no answer, but looked up steadfastly toward heaven, like Stephen, the first martyr, his eyes streaming with tears. He looked at me," said Sabat, "but it was with the countenance of forgiveness."

Abdallah's other arm was stretched out, again the sword flashed and fell. His other hand dropped to the ground. He stood there bleeding and handless. He bowed his head and his neck was bared to the sword. Again the blade flashed. He was beheaded, and Sabat--Sabat who had ridden a thousand miles with his friend and had faced with him the blistering sun of the desert and the snow-blizzard of the mountain--saw Abdallah's head lie there on the ground and the dead body carried away.

Abdallah had died because he was faithful to Jesus Christ and because Sabat had obeyed the law of Mohammed.

The Old Sabat and the New The news spread through Bokhara like a forest fire. They could hardly believe that a man would die for the Christian faith like that. As Sabat told his friends afterward, "All Bokhara seemed to say, 'What new thing is this?'"

But Sabat was in agony of mind. Nothing that he could do would take away from his eyes the vision of his friend's face as Abdallah had looked at him when his hands were being cut off. He plunged out on to the camel tracks of Asia to try to forget. He wandered far and he wandered long, but he could not forget or find rest for his tortured mind.

At last he sailed away on the seas and landed on the coast of India at Madras. The British East India Company then ruled in India, and they gave Sabat a post in the civil courts as mufti, _i.e._ as an expounder of the law of Mohammed. He spent most of his time in a coast town north of Madras, called Vizagapatam.[59] A friend handed to him there a little book in his native language--Arabic. It was another translation of those stories that Abdallah had read in Kabul--it was the New Testament.[60]

Sabat sat reading this New Book. He then took up the book of Mohammed's law--the Koran--which it was his daily work to explain. He compared the two. "The truth came"--as he himself said--"like a flood of light." He too began to worship Jesus Christ, whose life he had read now for the first time in the New Testament. Sabat decided that he must follow in Abdallah's footsteps. He became a Christian.[61] He was then twenty-seven years of age.

The Brother's Dagger

In the world of the East news travels like magic by Arab dhow (sailing ship) and camel caravan. Very quickly the news was in Arabia that Sabat had renounced Mohammed and become a Christian. At once Sabat's brother rose, girded on his dagger, left the tents of his tribe, mounted his camel and coursed across Arabia to a port. There he took ship for Madras. Landing, he disguised himself as an Indian and went up to Vizagapatam to the house where his brother Sabat was living.

Sabat saw this Indian, as he appeared to be, standing before him. He suspected nothing. Suddenly the disguised brother put his hand within his robe, seized his dagger, and leaping at Sabat made a fierce blow at him. Sabat flung out his arm. He spoilt his brother's aim, but he was too late to save himself. He was wounded, but not killed. The brother threw off his disguise, and Sabat--remembering the forgiveness of Abdallah--forgave his brother, gave him many presents, and sent loving messages to his mother.

Sabat decided that he could no longer work as an expounder of Moslem law: he wanted to do work that would help to spread the Christian Faith. He went away north to Calcutta, and there he joined the great men who were working at the task of translating the Bible into different languages and printing them. This work pleased Sabat, for was it not through reading an Arabic New Testament that all his own life had been changed?

Because Sabat knew Persian as well as Arabic he was sent to help a very clever young chaplain from England named Henry Martyn, who was busily at work translating the New Testament into Persian and Arabic. So Sabat went up the Ganges to Cawnpore with Henry Martyn.

Sabat's fiery temper nearly drove Martyn wild. His was a flaming Arab spirit, hot-headed and impetuous; yet he would be ready to die for the man he cared for; proud and often ignorant, yet simple--as Martyn said, "an artless child of the desert."

Sabat's knowledge of Persian was not really so good as he himself thought it was, and some of the Indian translators at Calcutta criticised his translation. At this he got furiously angry, and, like St. Peter, the fiery, impetuous apostle, he denied Jesus Christ and spoke against Christianity.

With his heart burning with rage and his great voice thundering with anger, Sabat left his friends, went aboard ship and sailed down the Bay of Bengal by the Indo-Chinese coast till he came to Penang, where he began to live as a trader.

But by this time the fire of his anger had burnt itself out. He--again like Peter--remembered his denial of his Master, and when he saw in a Penang newspaper an article saying that the famous Sabat, who had become a Christian and then become a Mohammedan again, had come to live in their city, he wrote a letter which was published in the newspaper at Penang declaring that he was now--and for good and all--a Christian.

A British officer named Colonel MacInnes was stationed at Penang. Sabat went to him. "My mind is full of great sorrow," he said, "because I denied Jesus Christ. I have not had a moment's peace since Satan made me do that bad work. I did it for revenge. I only want to do one thing with my life: to spend it in undoing this evil that has come through my denial."

Sabat left the house of the Mohammedan with whom he was living in

Penang. He found an old friend of his named Johannes, an Armenian Christian merchant, who had lived in Madras in the very days when Sabat first became a Christian. Every night Johannes the Armenian and Sabat the Arab got out their Bibles, and far into the night Sabat would explain their meaning to Johannes.

The Prince from Sumatra One day all Penang was agog with excitement because a brown Prince from Acheen, a Malay State in the island of Sumatra, had suddenly sailed into the harbour. He was in flight from his own land, where rebels had attacked him. The people of Acheen were wild and ferocious; many of them were cannibals.

"I will join you in helping to recover your throne," said Sabat to the fugitive Prince. "I am going," said Sabat to Colonel MacInnes, "to see if I can carry the message of Christianity to this fierce people."

So Sabat and the Prince, with others, went aboard a sailing ship and crossed the Strait of Malacca to Sumatra. They landed, and for long the struggle with the rebels swayed from side to side. The Prince was so pleased with Sabat that he made him his Prime Minister. But the struggle dragged on and on; there seemed to be no hope of triumph. At last Sabat decided to go back to Penang. One day he left the Prince and started off, but soldiers of the rebel-chief Syfoolalim captured him.

Great was the joy of the rebels--their powerful enemy was in their hands! They bound him, threw him into a boat, hoisted him aboard a sailing ship and clapped him in the stifling darkness of the hold. As he lay there he pierced his arm to make it bleed, and, with the blood that came out, wrote on a piece of paper that was smuggled out and sent to Penang to Colonel MacInnes.

The agonies that Sabat suffered in the gloom and filth of that ship's hold no one will ever know. We can learn from the words that he wrote in the blood from his own body that they loaded worse horrors upon him because he was a Christian. All the scene is black, but out of the darkness comes a voice that makes us feel that Sabat was faithful at the end. In his last letter to Colonel MacInnes he told how he was now ready (like his friend Abdallah) to die for the sake of that Master whom he had in his rage denied.

Then one day his cruel gaolers came to the hold where he lay, and, binding his limbs, thrust him into a sack, which they then closed. In the choking darkness of the sack he was carried on deck and dragged to the side of the ship. He heard the lapping of the waves. He felt himself lifted and then hurled out into the air, and down--down with a crash into the waters of the sea, which closed over him for ever.

FOOTNOTES:

[Footnote 58: The inn of the Near East--a square courtyard with all the doors and windows inside, with primitive stables and bunks for the camelmen, and sometimes rooms for the well-to-do travellers.]

[Footnote 59: Pronounce Vi-zah'-ga-pat-ahm.]

[Footnote 60: The Arabic New Testament revised by Solomon Negri and sent to India by the Society for the Promotion of Christian Knowledge in the middle of the eighteenth century.]

[Footnote 61: Baptized "Nathaniel" at Madras by the Rev. Dr Kerr.]

CHAPTER XXIV

A RACE AGAINST TIME

Henry Martyn (Dates, b. 1781, d. 1812. Time of Incident 1810-12)

In the story of Sabat that was told in the previous chapter you will remember that, for a part of the time that he lived in India, he worked with an Englishman named Henry Martyn.

Sabat was almost a giant; Henry Martyn was slight and not very strong. Yet-- as we shall see in the story that follows--Henry Martyn was braver and more constant than Sabat himself.

As a boy Henry, who was born and went to school in Truro, in Cornwall, in the West of England, was violently passionate, sensitive, and physically rather fragile, and at school was protected from bullies by a big boy, the son of

Admiral Kempthorne.

He left school at the age of fifteen and shot and read till he was seventeen. In 1797 he became an undergraduate at St. John's College, Cambridge. He was still very passionate.

For instance, when a man was "ragging" him in the College Hall at dinner, he was so furious that he flung a knife at him, which stuck quivering in the panelling of the wall. Kempthorne, his old friend, was at Cambridge with him. They used to read the Bible together and Martyn became a real Christian and fought hard to overcome his violent temper.

He was a very clever scholar and became a Fellow of Jesus College in 1802. He at that time took orders in the Church of England. He became very keen on reading about missionary work, e.g. Carey's story of nine years' work in Periodical Accounts, and the L.M.S. Report on Vanderkemp in South Africa. "I read nothing else while it lasted," he said of the Vanderkemp report.

He was accepted as a chaplain of the East India Company. They could not sail till Admiral Nelson gave the word, because the French were waiting to capture all the British ships. Five men-of-war convoyed them when they sailed in 1805. They waited off Ireland, because the immediate invasion of England by Napoleon was threatened. On board Martyn worked hard at Hindustani, Bengali and Portuguese. He already knew Greek, Latin and Hebrew. He arrived at Madras (South India) and Calcutta and thence went to Cawnpore. It is at this point that our yarn begins.

A voice like thunder, speaking in a strange tongue, shouted across an Indian garden one night in 1809.

The new moon, looking "like a ball of ebony in an ivory cup,"--as one who was there that night said--threw a cold light over the palm trees and aloes, on the man who was speaking and on those who were seated around him at the table in the bungalow.

Beyond the garden the life of Cawnpore moved in its many streets; the shout of a donkey-driver, the shrill of a bugle from the barracks broke sharply through the muffled sounds of the city. The June wind, heavy with the waters of the Ganges which flows past Cawnpore, made the night insufferably hot. But the heat did not trouble Sabat, the wild son of the Arabian desert, who was talking--as he always did--in a roaring voice that was louder than most men's shouting. He was telling the story of Abdallah's brave death as a Christian martyr.[62]

Quietly listening to Sabat's voice--though he could not understand what he was saying--was a young Italian, Padre Julius C鍹ar, a monk of the order of the Jesuits. On his head was a little skull-cap, over his body a robe of fine purple satin held with a girdle of twisted silk.

Near him sat an Indian scholar--on his dark head a full turban, and about him richly-coloured robes. On the other side sat a little, thin, copper-coloured Bengali dressed in white, and a British officer in his scarlet and gold uniform, with his wife, who has told us the story of that evening.

Not one of these brightly dressed people was, however, the strongest power there. A man in black clothes was the real centre of the group. Very slight in build, not tall, clean-shaven, with a high forehead and sensitive lips, young Henry Martyn seemed a stripling beside the flaming Arab. Yet Sabat, with all his sound and fury, was no match for the swift-witted, clear-brained young Englishman. Henry Martyn was a chaplain in the army of the East India Company, which then ruled in India.

He was the only one of those who were listening to Sabat who could understand what he was saying. When Sabat had finished his story, Martyn turned, and, in his clear, musical voice translated it from the Persian into Latin mixed with Italian for Padre Julius C鍹ar, into Hindustani for the Indian scholar, into Bengali for the Bengal gentleman, and into English for the British officer and his wife. Martyn could also talk to Sabat himself both in Arabic and in Persian.

As Martyn listened to the rolling sentences of Sabat, the Christian Arab, he seemed to see the lands beyond India, away across the Khyber Pass, where Sabat had travelled--Mesopotamia, Arabia, Persia.

Henry Martyn knew that in all those lands the people were Mohammedans. He wanted one thing above everything else in the world: that was to give them all the chance of doing what Sabat and Abdallah had done--the chance of reading in their own languages the one book in the world that could tell them that God was a Father--the book of letters and of biographies that we call the New Testament.

The Toil of Brain There was not in the world a copy of the New Testament in good Persian. To make one Henry Martyn slaved hard, far into the hot, sultry Indian nights, with scores of mosquitoes "pinging" round his lamp and his head, grinding at his Persian grammar, so that he could translate the life of Jesus Christ into that language.

Even while he was listening to Sabat's story in the bungalow at Cawnpore, Martyn knew that he was so ill that he could not live for many years more. The doctor said that he must leave India for a time to be in a healthier place. Should he go home to England, where all his friends were? He wanted that; but much more he wanted to go on with his work. So he asked the doctor if he might go to Persia on the way home, and he agreed.

So Martyn went down from Cawnpore to Calcutta, and in a boat down the Hoogli river to the little Arab coasting sailing ship the Hummoudi, which hoisted sail and started on its voyage round India to Bombay. Martyn read while on board the Old Testament in the original Hebrew and the New Testament in the original Greek, so that he might understand them better and make a more perfect translation into Persian. He read the Koran of Mohammed so that he could argue with the Persians about it. And he worked hard at Arabic grammar, and read books in Persian. Yet he was for ever cracking jokes with his fellow travellers, cooped up in the little ship on the hot tropical seas.

From Bombay the governor granted Martyn a passage up the Persian Gulf in the Benares, a ship in the Indian Navy that was going on a cruise to finish the exciting work of hunting down the fierce Arab pirates of the Persian Gulf. So on Lady Day, 1811, the sailors got her under weigh and tacked northward up the Gulf, till at last, on May 21, the roofs and minarets of Bushire hove in sight. Martyn, leaning over the bulwarks, could see the town jutting out into the Gulf on a spit of sand and the sea almost surrounding it. That day he set foot for the first time on the soil of Persia.

Across Persia on a Pony Aboard ship Martyn had allowed his beard and moustache to grow. When he landed at Bushire he bought and wore the clothes of a Persian gentleman, so that he should escape from attracting everybody's notice by wearing clothes such as the people had never seen before.

No one who had seen the pale, clean-shaven clergyman in black silk coat and trousers in Cawnpore would have recognised the Henry Martyn who rode out that night on his pony with an Armenian servant, Zechariah of Isfahan, on his long one hundred and seventy mile journey from Bushire to Shiraz. He wore a conical cap of black Astrakhan fur, great baggy trousers of blue, bright red leather boots, a light tunic of chintz, and over that a flowing cloak.

They went out through the gates of Bushire on to the great plain of burning sand that stretched away for ninety miles ahead of them. They travelled by night, because the day was intolerably hot, but even at midnight the heat was over 100 degrees. It was a fine moonlight night; the stars sparkled over the plain. The bells tinkled on the mules' necks as they walked across the sand. All else was silent.

At last dawn broke. Martyn pitched his little tent under a tree, the only shelter he could get. Gradually the heat grew more and more intense. He was already so ill that it was difficult to travel.

"When the thermometer was above 112 degrees--fever heat," says Martyn, "I began to lose my strength fast. It became intolerable. I wrapped myself up in a blanket and all the covering I could get to defend myself from the air. By this means the moisture was kept a little longer upon the body. I thought I should have lost my senses. The thermometer at last stood at 126 degrees. I concluded that death was inevitable."

At last the sun went down: the thermometer crept lower: it was night and time to start again. But Martyn had not slept or eaten. He could hardly sit upright on his pony. Yet he set out and travelled on through the night.

Next morning he had a little shelter of leaves and branches made, and an Arab poured water on the leaves and on Martyn all day to try to keep some of the frightful heat from him. But even then the heat almost slew him. So they marched on through another night and then camped under a grove of date palms.

"I threw myself on the burning ground and slept," Martyn wrote. "When the tent came up I awoke in a burning fever. All day I had recourse to the wet towel, which kept me alive, but would allow of no sleep."

At nine that night they struck camp. The ground threw up the heat that it had taken from the sun during the day. So frightfully hot was the air that even at midnight Martyn could not travel without a wet towel round his face and neck.

As the night drew on the plain grew rougher: then it began to rise to the foothills and mountains. At last the pony and mules were clambering up rough steep paths so wild that there was (as Martyn said) "nothing to mark the road but the rocks being a little more worn in one place than in another." Suddenly in the darkness the pony stopped; dimly through the gloom Martyn could see that they were on the edge of a tremendous precipice. A single step more would have plunged him over, to be smashed on the rocks hundreds of feet below. Martyn did not move or try to guide the beast: he knew that the pony himself was the safest guide. In a minute or two the animal moved, and step by step clambered carefully up the rock-strewn mountain-side.

At last they came out on the mountain top, but only to find that they were on the edge of a flat high plain--a tableland. The air was pure and fresher; the mules and the travellers revived. Martyn's pony began to trot briskly along. So, as dawn came up, they came in sight of a great courtyard built by the king of that country to refresh pilgrims.

Through night after night they tramped, across plateau and mountain range, till they climbed the third range, and then plunged by a winding rocky path into a wide valley where, at a great town called Kazrun, in a garden of cypress trees was a summer-house.

Martyn lay down on the floor but could not sleep, though he was horribly weary. "There seemed," he said, "to be fire within my head, my skin like a cinder." His heart beat like a hammer.

They went on climbing another range of mountains, first tormented by mosquitoes, then frozen with cold; Martyn was so overwhelmed with sleep that he could not sit on his pony and had to hurry ahead to keep awake and then sit down with his back against a rock where he fell asleep in a second, and had to be shaken to wake up when Zechariah, the Armenian mule driver, came up to where he was.

They had at last climbed the four mountain rungs of the ladder to Persia, and came out on June 11th, 1811, on the great plain where the city of Shiraz stands. Here he found the host Jaffir Ali Khan, to whom he carried his letters of introduction. Martyn in his Persian dress, seated on the ground, was feasted with curries and rice, sweets cooled with snow and perfumed with rose water, and coffee.

Ali Khan had a lovely garden of orange trees, and in the garden Martyn sat. Ill as he was, he worked day in and day out to translate the life of Jesus Christ in the New Testament from the Greek language into pure and simple Persian. The kind host put up a tent for Martyn in the garden, close to some beautiful vines, from which hung lovely bunches of purple grapes. By the side of his tent ran a clear stream of running water. All the evening nightingales sang sweetly and mournfully.

As he sat there at his work, men came hundreds of miles to talk with this holy man, as they felt him to be. Moslems--they yet travelled even from Baghdad and Bosra and Isfahan to hear this "infidel" speak of Jesus Christ, and to argue as to which was the true religion. Prince Abbas Mirza invited him to come to speak with him; and as Martyn entered the Prince's courtyard a hundred fountains began to send up jets of water in his honour.

At last they came to him in such numbers that Martyn was obliged to say to many of them that he could not see them. He hated sending them away. What was it forced him to do so?

The Race against Time It was because he was running a race against time. He knew that he could not live very long, because the disease that had smitten his lungs was gaining ground every day. And the thing that he had come to Persia for--the object that had made him face the long voyage, the frightful heat and the freezing cold of the journey, the life thousands of miles from his home in Cornwall--was that he might finish such a translation of the New Testament into Persian that men should love to read years and years after he had died.

So each day Martyn finished another page or two of the book, written in lovely Persian letters. He began the work within a week of reaching Shiraz, and in seven months (February, 1812) it was finished. Three more months were spent in writing out very beautiful copies of the whole of the New Testament in this new translation, to be presented to the Shah of Persia and to the heir to the throne, Prince Abbas Mirza.

Then he started away on a journey right across Persia to find the Shah and Prince so that he might give his precious books to them. On the way he fell ill with great fever; he was so weak and giddy that he could not stand. One night his head ached so that it almost drove him mad; he shook all over with fever; then a great sweat broke out. He was almost unconscious with weakness, but at midnight when the call came to start he mounted his horse and, as he says, "set out, rather dead than alive." So he pressed on in great weakness till he reached Tabriz, and there met the British Ambassador.

Martyn was rejoiced, and felt that all his pains were repaid when Sir Gore Ouseley said that he himself would present the Sacred Book to the Shah and the Prince. When the day came to give the book to Prince Abbas, poor Henry Martyn was so weak that he could not rise from his bed. Before the other copy could be presented to the Shah, Martyn had died. This is how it came about.

The Last Trail His great work was done. The New Testament was finished. He sent a copy to the printers in India. He could now go home to England and try to get well again. He started out on horseback with two Armenian servants and a Turkish guide. He was making along the old track that has been the road from Asia to Europe for thousands of years. His plan was to travel across Persia, through Armenia and over the Black Sea to Constantinople, and so back to England.

For forty-five days he moved on, often going as much as ninety miles, and generally as much as sixty in a day. He slept in filthy inns where fleas and lice abounded and mosquitoes tormented him. Horses, cows, buffaloes and sheep would pass through his sleeping-room, and the stench of the stables nearly poisoned him. Yet he was so ill that often he could hardly keep his seat on his horse.

He travelled through deep ravines and over high mountain passes and across vast plains. His head ached till he felt it would split; he could not eat; fever came on. He shook with ague. Yet his remorseless Turkish guide, Hassan, dragged him along, because he wanted to get the journey over and go back home.

At last one day Martyn got rest on damp ground in a hovel, his eyes and forehead feeling as though a great fire burnt in them. "I was almost frantic," he wrote. Martyn was, in fact, dying; yet Hassan compelled him to ride a hundred and seventy miles of mountain track to Tokat. Here, on October 6th, 1812, he wrote in his journal:

"No horses to be had, I had an unexpected repose. I sat in the orchard and thought with sweet comfort and peace of my God--in solitude my Company, my Friend, my Comforter."

It was the last word he was ever to write.

Alone, without a human friend by him, he fell asleep. But the book that he had written with his life-blood, the Persian New Testament, was printed, and has told thousands of Persians in far places, where no Christian man has penetrated, that story of the love of God that is shown in Jesus Christ.

FOOTNOTES:

[Footnote 62: See Chapter XXIII.]

CHAPTER XXV

THE MOSES OF THE ASSYRIANS

William Ambrose Shedd (1865-1918)

I

A dark-haired American with black, penetrating eyes that looked you steadily in the face, and sparkled with light when he laughed, sat on a chair in a hall in 1918 in the ancient city of Urumia in the land of Assyria where Persia and Turkey meet.

His face was as brown with the sunshine of this eastern land as were the wrinkled faces of the turbaned Assyrian village men who stood before him. For he was born out here in Persia on Mount Seir.[63] And he had lived here as a boy and a man, save for the time when his splendid American father had sent him to Marietta, Ohio, for some of his schooling, and to Princeton for his final training. His dark brown moustache and short beard covered a firm mouth and a strong chin. His vigorous expression and his strongly Roman nose added to the commanding effect of his presence.

A haunting terror had driven these ragged village people into the city of Urumia, to ask help of this wonderful American leader whom they almost worshipped because he was so strong and just and good.

For the bloodthirsty Turks and the even more cruel and wilder Kurds of the mountains were marching on the land. The Great War was raging across the world and even the hidden peoples of this distant mountain land were swept into its terrible flames.

For Urumia city lies to the west of the southern end of the extremely salt lake of the same name. It is about 150 miles west from the Caspian Sea and the same distance north of the site of ancient Nineveh. It stands on a small plain and in that tangle of lakes, mountains and valley-plains where the ambitions of Russia, Persia and Turkey have met, and where the Assyrians (Christians of one of the most ancient churches in the world, which in the early centuries had a chain of missions from Constantinople right across Asia to Peking), the Kurds (wild, fierce Moslems), the Persians, the Turks and the Russians struggled together.

In front of Dr. William Ambrose Shedd there stood an old man from the villages. His long grey hair and beard and his wrinkled face were agitated as he told the American his story. The old man's dress was covered with patches--an eyewitness counted thirty-seven patches--all of different colours on one side of his cloak and loose baggy trousers.

"My field in my village I cannot plough," he said, "for we have no ox. The Kurds have taken our possessions, you are our father. Grant us an ox to plough and draw for us."

Dr. Shedd saw that the old man spoke truth; he scribbled a few words on a slip of paper and the old man went out satisfied.

So for hour after hour, men and women from all the country round came to this strange missionary who had been asked by the American Government to administer relief, yes, and to be the Consul representing America itself in that great territory.

They came to him from the villages where, around the fire in the Khans at night, men still tell stories of him as one of the great hero-leaders of their race. These are the kind of stories that they tell of the courage and the gentleness of this man who--while he was a fine American scholar--yet knew the very heart of the Eastern peoples in northwestern Persia as no American has ever done in all our history.

"One day," says one old village Assyrian greybeard, "Dr. Shedd was sitting at meat in his house when his servant, Meshadi, ran into the room crying, 'The Kurds have been among our people. They have taken three girls, three Christian girls, and are carrying them off. They have just passed the gate.' The Kurds were all bristling with daggers and pistols. Dr. Shedd simply picked up the cane that he holds in his hand when he walks. He hurried out of the house with Meshadi, ran up the hill to the Kurd village that lies there, entered, said to the fierce Kurds, 'Give back those girls to us.' And they, as they looked into his face, could not resist him though they were armed and he was not. So they gave the Assyrian girls back to him and he led them down the hill to their homes."

So he also stood single-handed between Turks and five hundred Assyrians who had taken refuge in the missionary compound, and stopped the Turks from massacring the Christians.

But even as he worked in this way the tide of the great war flowed towards

Urumia. The people there were mostly Assyrians with some Armenians; they were Christians. They looked southward across the mountains to the British Army there in Mesopotamia for aid.

But, as the Assyrians looked up from Urumia to the north they could already see the first Turks coming down upon the city. Thousands upon thousands of the Assyrians from the country villages crowded into the city and into the American missionary compound, till actually even in the mission school-rooms they were sleeping three deep--one lot on the floor, another lot on the seats of the desks and a third on the top of the desks themselves.

"Hold on; resist; the help of the British will come," said Dr. Shedd to the people. "Agha Petros with a thousand of our men has gone to meet the British and he will come back with them and will throw back the Turks."

The Turks and the Kurds came on from the north; many of the Armenian and Assyrian men were out across the plains to the east getting in the harvest; and no sign of succour came from the south.

II

Through the fierce hot days of July the people held on because Dr. Shedd said that they must; but at last on the afternoon of July 30th there came over all the people a strange irresistible panic. They gathered all their goods together and piled them in wagons--food, clothes, saucepans, jewelry, gold, silver, babies, old women, mothers,--all were huddled and jumbled together.

The wagons creaked, the oxen lurched down the roads to the south, the little children cried with hunger and fright, the boys trudged along rather excited at the adventure yet rather scared at the awful hullabaloo and the strange feeling of horror of the cruel Kurdish horsemen and of the crafty Turk.

Dr. Shedd made one last vain effort to persuade the people to hold on to their city; but it was impossible--they had gone, as it seemed, mad with fright.

He and his wife went to bed that night but not to sleep. At two o'clock the telephone bell rang.

"The Turks and Kurds are advancing; all the people are leaving," came the message.

"It is impossible to hold on any longer," said Dr. Shedd to his wife. "I will go and tell all in the compound. You get things ready."

Mrs. Shedd got up and began to collect what was needed: she packed up food (bread, tea, sugar, nuts, raisins and so on), a frying pan, a kettle, a saucepan, water jars, saddles, extra horse-shoes, ropes, lanterns, a spade and bedding. By 7.30 the baggage wagon and two Red Cross carts were ready. Dr. Shedd and Mrs. Shedd got up into the wagon; the driver cried to his horses and they started.

As they went out of the city on the south the Turks and Kurds came raging in on the north. Within two hours the Turks and Kurds were crashing into houses and burning them to the ground; but most of the people had gone-- for Dr. Shedd was practically the last to leave Urumia.

Ahead of them were the Armenians and Syrians in flight. They came to a little bridge--a mass of sticks with mud thrown over them. Here, and at every bridge, pandemonium reigned. This is how Mrs. Shedd describes the scene:

"The jam at every bridge was indescribable confusion. Every kind of vehicle that you could imagine--ox carts, buffalo wagons, Red Cross carts, troikas, foorgans like prairie schooners, hay-wagons, Russian pha 雖 ons and many others invented and fitted up for the occasion. The animals--donkeys, horses, buffaloes, oxen, cows with their calves, mules and herds of thousands of sheep and goats."

All through the day they moved on, at the end of the procession--Dr. Shedd, planning out how he could best get his people safely away from the Turks who--he knew--would soon come pursuing them down the plain to the mountains. Night fell and they were in a long line of wagons close to a narrow bridge built by the Russians across the Baranduz river. They had come some eighteen miles from Urumia.

So they lay down in the wagons to try to sleep. But they could not and at two o'clock in the night they moved on, crossed the river and drove on for hour after hour toward the mountains that rose in a wall before them.

The poor horses were not strong so the wagon had to be lightened. Assyrian boys took loads on their heads and trudged up the rocky mountain road while the wagon jolted and groaned as it bumped its way along. The trail of the mountain pass was littered with samovars (tea urns), copper kettles, carpets, bedding; and here and there the body of someone who had died on the way. At the very top of the pass lay a baby thrown aside there and just drawing its last breath.

So for two days they jolted on hardly getting an hour's sleep. At last at midday on the third day they left Hadarabad at the south end of Lake Urumia. Two hours later the sound of booming guns was heard. A horseman galloped up.

"The Turks are in Hadarabad," he said. "They are attacking the rear of the procession."

"It seemed," said Mrs. Shedd, "as if at any moment we should hear the screams of those behind, as the enemy fell upon them."

The wagons hurried on to the next town called Memetyar and there Dr. Shedd waited, lightening his own wagons by throwing away everything that they could spare--oil, potatoes, charcoal, every box except his Bible and a small volume of Browning's Poems.

Then they started again, along a road that was littered with the discarded goods of the people. Then they saw on the road-side a little baby girl that had been left by her parents. She was not a year old and sat there all alone in a desolate spot. Left to die. Dr. Shedd looked at his wife and she at him.

He pulled up the horse and jumped down, picked up the baby and put her in the wagon. They went along till they came to a large village. Here they found a Kurdish mother.

"Take care of this little girl till we come back," said Dr. Shedd, "and here is some money for looking after her. We will give you more when we come back if she is well looked after."

III

Suddenly cannon were fired from the mountains and the people in panic threw away their goods and hurried in a frenzy of fear down the mountain passes. They passed on to the plain, and then as they were in a village guns began to be fired. Three hundred Turks and Persians were attacking under Majdi--Sultana of Urumia. Dr. Shedd, riding his horse, gathered together some Armenian and Assyrian men with guns and stayed with them to help them hold back the enemy, while the women drove on. He was a good target sitting up there on his horse; but without thinking of his own danger he kept his men at it. For he felt like a shepherd with a great flock of fleeing sheep whom it was his duty to protect.

Panic seized the people. Strong men left their old mothers to die. Mothers dropped their babies and ran.

"One of my school-girls," Mrs. Shedd says, "afterward told me how she had left her baby on the bank and waded with an older child through the river when the enemy were coming after them. She couldn't carry both. The memory of her deserted baby is always with her."

The line of the refugees stretched for miles along the road. The enemy fired from behind boulders on the mountain sides. The Armenians and Syrians fired back from the road or ran up the mountains to chase them. It was hopeless to think of driving the enemy off but Dr. Shedd's object was to hold them off till help came. So he went up and down on his horse encouraging the men; while the bullets whizzed over the wagons.

"I feared," said Mrs. Shedd, "that the enemy might get the better of us and we should have to leave the carts and run for our lives. While they were plundering the wagons and the loads we would get away. I looked about me to see what we might carry. There was little May, six years old (the daughter of one of their Syrian teachers) who had unconcernedly curled herself up on the seat for a nap. I wrapped a little bread in a cloth, put my glasses in my pocket, and took the bag of money so that I should be ready on a moment's notice for Dr. Shedd if they should swoop down upon us."

All day long the firing went on from the mountain side as the tired horses pulled along the rough trail. The sun began to sink toward the horizon. What would happen in the darkness?

Then they saw ahead of them coming from the south a group of men in khaki. They were nine British Tommies with three Lewis guns under Captain Savage. They had come ahead from the main body that had moved up from Baghdad in order to defend the rear of the great procession. The little company of soldiers passed on and the procession moved forward. That tiny company of nine British Tommies ten miles farther on was attacked by hundreds of Turks. All day they held the road, like Horatius on the bridge, till at night the Cavalry came up and drove off the enemy, and at last the Shedds reached the British camp.

"Why are you right at the tail end of the retreat?" asked one of the Syrian young men who had hurried forward into safety.

"I would much rather be there," said Dr. Shedd with some scorn in his voice, "than like you, leave the unarmed, the sick, the weak, the women and the children to the mercy of the enemy."

He was rejoiced that the British had come.

"There was," said Mrs. Shedd, "a ring in his voice, a light in his eyes, a buoyancy in his step that I had not seen for months."

He had shepherded his thousands and thousands of boys and girls, and men and women through the mountains into the protection of the British squadron of troops.

IV

Later that day Dr. Shedd began to feel the frightful heat of the August day so exhausting that he had to lie down in the cart, which had a canvas cover open at both ends and was therefore much cooler than a tent. He got more and more feverish. So Mrs. Shedd got the Assyrian boys to take out the baggage and she made up a bed for him on the floor of the cart.

The English doctor was out with the cavalry who were holding back and dispersing the Turkish force.

Then a British officer came and said: "We are moving the camp forward under the protection of the mountains."

It was late afternoon. The cart moved forward into the gathering darkness. Mrs. Shedd crouched beside her husband on the floor of the cart attending to him, expecting the outriders to tell her when they came to the British Camp.

For hours the cart rolled and jolted over the rough mountain roads. At last it stopped, it was so dark they could not see the road. They were in a gully and could not go forward.

"Where is the British camp?" asked Mrs. Shedd.

"We passed it miles back on the road," was the reply.

It was a terrible blow: the doctor, the medicines, the comfort, the nursing that would have helped Dr. Shedd were all miles away and he was so ill that it was impossible to drive him back over that rough mountain track in the inky darkness of the night.

There was nothing to do but just stay where they were, send a messenger to the camp for the doctor, and wait for the morning.

"Only a few drops of oil were left in the lantern," Mrs. Shedd tells us, "but I lighted it and looked at Mr. Shedd. I could see that he was very sick indeed and asked two of the men to go back for the doctor. It was midnight before the doctor reached us.

"The men," Mrs. Shedd continues, "set fire to a deserted cart left by the refugees and this furnished fire and light all night. They arranged for guards in turn and lay down to rest on the roadside. Hour after hour I crouched in the cart beside my husband massaging his limbs when cramps attacked him, giving him water frequently, for while he was very cold to the touch, he seemed feverish. We heated the hot water bottle for his feet, and made coffee for him at the blaze; we had no other nourishment. He got weaker and weaker, and a terrible fear tugged at my heart.

"Fifty thousand hunted, terror-stricken refugees had passed on; the desolate, rocky mountains loomed above us, darkness was all about us and heaven seemed too far away for prayer to reach. A deserted baby wailed all night not far away. When the doctor came he gave two hypodermic injections and returned to the camp saying we should wait there for him to catch up to us in the morning. After the injections Mr. Shedd rested better but he did not again regain consciousness.

"When the light began to reveal things, I could see the awful change in his face, but I could not believe that he was leaving me. Shortly after light the men told me that we could not wait as they heard fighting behind and it was evident the English were attacked, so in his dying hour we had to take him over the rough, stony road. After an hour or two Capt. Reed and the doctor caught up to us. We drew the cart to the side of the road where soon he drew a few short, sharp breaths--and I was alone."

So the British officers, with a little hoe, on the mountain side dug the grave of this brave American shepherd, who had given his life in defending the Assyrian flock from the Turkish wolf. They made the grave just above the road beside a rock; and on it they sprinkled dead grass so that it might not be seen and polluted by the enemy.

* * * * *

The people Dr. Shedd loved were safe. The enemy, whose bullets he had braved for day after day, was defeated by the British soldiers. But the great American leader, whose tired body had not slept while the Assyrians and Armenians were being hunted through the mountains, lies there dreamless on the mountain side.

These are words that broke from the lips of Assyrian sheiks when they heard of his death:

"He bore the burdens of the whole nation upon his shoulders to the last breath of his life.

"As long as we obeyed his advice and followed his lead we were safe and prosperous, but when we ceased to do that destruction came upon us. He was, and ever will be, the Moses of the Assyrian people."

He lies there where his heart always was--in that land in which the Turk, the Assyrian, the Armenian, the Persian, the Russian and the Arab meet; he is there waiting for the others who will go out and take up the work that he has left, the work of carrying to all those eastern peoples the love of the Christ whom Dr. Shedd died in serving.

FOOTNOTES:

[Footnote 63: Born January 25th, 1865. Graduated Marietta College, Ohio, 1887, and Princeton Theological Seminary, 1892.]

CHAPTER XXVI

AN AMERICAN NURSE IN THE GREAT WAR

E.D. Cushman

(Time 1914-1920)

The Turk in Bed The cold, clear sunlight of a winter morning on the high plateau of Asia Minor shone into the clean, white ward of a hospital in Konia (the greatest city in the heart of that land). The hospital in which the events that I am going to tell in this story happened is supported by Christian folk in America, and was established by two American medical missionaries, Dr. William S. Dodd, and Dr. Wilfred Post, with Miss Cushman, the head nurse, sharing the general superintendence: other members of the staff are Haralambos, their Armenian dispenser and druggist, and Kleoniki, a Greek nurse trained by Miss Cushman. The author spent the early spring of 1914 at the hospital in Konia, when all the people named above were at work there.

The tinkle of camel-bells as a caravan of laden beasts swung by, the quick pad-pad of donkeys' hoofs, the howl of a Turkish dog, the cry of a child--these and other sounds of the city came through the open window of the ward.

On a bed in the corner of the ward lay a bearded man--a Turk--who lived in this ancient city of Konia (the Iconium of St. Paul's day). His brown face and grizzled beard were oddly framed in the white of the spotless pillow and sheets.

His face turned to the door as it opened and the matron entered. The eyes of the Turk as he lay there followed her as she walked toward one of her deft, gentle-handed assistant nurses who, in their neat uniforms with their olive-brown faces framed in dark hair, went from bed to bed tending the patients; giving medicine to a boy here, shaking up a pillow for a sick man there, taking a patient's temperature yonder. Those skilled nurses were Armenian girls. The Armenians are a Christian nation, who have been ruled by the Turks for centuries and often have been massacred by them; yet these Armenian girls were nursing the Turks in the hospital. But the matron of the hospital was not a Turk, nor an Armenian. She had come four thousand miles across the sea to heal the Turks and the Armenians in this land. She was an American.

The Turk in bed turned his eyes from the nurses to a picture on the wall. A frown came on his face. He began to mutter angry words into his beard.

As a Turk he had always been taught, even as a little boy, that the great Prophet Mohammed had told them they must have no pictures of prophets, and he knew from what he had heard that the picture on the wall showed the face of a prophet. It was a picture of a man with a kind, strong face, dressed in garments of the lands of the East, and wearing a short beard. He was stooping down healing a little child. It was our Lord Jesus Christ the Great Physician.

As Miss Cushman--for that was the name of the matron--moved toward his bed, the Turk burst into angry speech.

"Have that picture taken down," he said roughly, pointing to it. She turned to look at the picture and then back at him, and said words like these: "No, that is the picture of Jesus, the great Doctor who lived long ago and taught the people that God is Love. It is because He taught that, and has called me to follow in His steps, that I am here to help to heal you."

But the Turk, who was not used to having women disobey his commands, again ordered angrily that the picture should be taken down. But the American missionary-nurse said gently, but firmly: "No, the picture must stay there to remind us of Jesus. If you cannot endure to see the picture there, then if you wish you may leave the hospital, of course."

And so she passed on. The Turk lay in his bed and thought it over. He wished to get well. If the doctors in this hospital--Dr. Dodd and Dr. Post--did not attend him, and if the nurses did not give him his medicine, he would not. He therefore decided to make no more fuss about the picture. So he lay looking at it, and was rather surprised to find in a few days that he liked to see it there, and that he wanted to hear more and more about the great Prophet-Doctor, Jesus.

Then he had another tussle of wills with Miss Cushman, the white nurse from across the seas. It came about in this way. Women who are Mohammedans keep their faces veiled, but the Armenian Christian nurses had their faces uncovered.

"Surely they are shameless women," he thought in his heart. "And they are Armenians too--Christian infidels!" So he began to treat them rudely. But the white nurse would not stand that.

Miss Cushman went and stood by his bed and said: "I want you to remember that these nurses of mine are here to help you to get well. They are to you even as daughters tending their father; and you must behave to them as a good father to good daughters."

So the Turk lay in bed and thought about that also. It took him a long time to take it in, for he had always been taught to hate the Armenians and to think low thoughts about their womenfolk. But in the end he learnt that lesson also.

At last the Turk got well, left his bed, and went away. He was so thankful that he was better that he was ready to do just anything in the world that Miss Cushman wanted him to do. The days passed on in the hospital, and always the white nurse from across the seas and the Armenian nurses tended the Turkish and other patients, and healed them through the heats of that summer.

War and Massacre As summer came near to its end there broke on the world the dreadful day when all Europe went to war. Miss Cushman's colleagues, the American doctors at the hospital, left Konia for service in the war. Soon Turkey entered the war. The fury of the Turks against the Armenians burst out into a flame. You might see in Konia two or three Turks sitting in the shadow of a little saddler's shop by the street smoking their hubble-bubble water-pipes, and saying words like these:

"The Armenians are plotting to help the enemies of Turkey. We shall have to kill them all."

"Yes, wipe them out--the accursed infidels!"

The Turks hate the Armenians because their religion, Islam, teaches them to hate the "infidel" Christians; they are of a foreign race and foreign religion in countries ruled by Turks, though the Armenians were there first, and the Armenians are cleverer business men than the Turks, who hate to see their subjects richer than themselves, and hope by massacre to seize Armenian wealth.

Yet all the time, as the wounded Turks were sent from the Gallipoli front back to Konia, the Armenian nurses in the hospital there were healing them. But the Turkish Government gave its orders. Vile bands of Turkish soldiers rushed down on the different cities and villages of the Armenians.[64] One sunny morning a troop of Turkish soldiers came dashing into a quiet little Armenian town among the hills. An order was given. The Turks smashed in the doors of the houses. A father stood up before his family; a bayonet was driven through him and soldiers dashed over his dead body; they looted the house; they smashed up his home; others seized the mother and the daughters--the mother had a baby in her arms; the baby was flung on the ground and then picked up dead on the point of a bayonet; and, though the mother and daughters were not bayoneted then, it would have been better to die at once than to suffer the unspeakable horrors that came to them.

And that happened in hundreds of villages and cities to hundred of thousands of Armenians, while hundreds of thousands more scattered down the mountain passes in flight towards Konia.

The Orphan Boys and Girls As Miss Cushman and her Armenian nurses looked out through the windows of the hospital, their hearts were sad as they saw some of these Armenian refugees trailing along the road like walking skeletons. What was to happen to them? It was very dangerous for anyone to show that they were friends with the Armenians, but the white matron was as brave as she was kind; so she went out to do what she could to help them.

One day she saw a little boy so thin that the bones seemed almost to be coming through his skin. He was very dirty; his hair was all matted together; and there were bugs and fleas in his clothes and in his hair. The hospital was so full that not another could be taken in. But the boy would certainly die if he were not looked after properly. His father and his mother had both been slain by the Turks; he did not know where his brothers were. He was an orphan alone in all the world.

Miss Cushman knew Armenian people in Konia, and she went to one of these homes and told them about the poor boy and arranged to pay them some money for the cost of his food. So she made a new home for him. The next day she found another boy, and then a girl, and so she went on and on, discovering little orphan Armenian boys and girls who had nobody to care for them, and finding them homes--until she had over six hundred orphans being cared for. It is certain that nearly all of them would have died if she had not looked after them.

So Miss Cushman gathered the six hundred Armenian children together into an orphanage, that was half for the boys and half for the girls. She was a hundred times better than the "Woman who Lived in a Shoe," because, though she had so many children, she did know what to do. She taught them to make nearly everything for themselves. In the mornings you would see half the boys figuring away at their sums or learning to write and read, while the other boys were hammering and sawing and planing at the carpenter's bench; cutting leather and sewing it to make shoes for the other boys and girls; cutting petrol tins up into sheets to solder into kettles and saucepans; and cutting and stitching cloth to make clothes. A young American Red Cross officer who went to see them wrote home, "The kids look happy and healthy and as clean as a whistle."

The People on the Plain As Miss Cushman looked out again from the hospital window she saw men coming from the country into the city jogging along on little donkeys.

"In the villages all across the plain," they said to her, "are Armenian boys and girls, and men and women. They are starving. Many are without homes, wandering about in rags till they simply lie down on the ground, worn out, and die."

Miss Cushman sent word to friends far away in America, and they sent food from America to Turkey in ships, and a million dollars of money to help the starving children. So Miss Cushman got together her boys and girls and some other helpers, and soon they were very busy all day and every day wrapping food and clothes into parcels.

Next a caravan of snorting camels came swinging in to the courtyard and, grumbling and rumbling, knelt down, to be loaded up. The parcels were done up in big bales and strapped on to the camels' backs. Then at a word from the driver the camels rose from their knees and went lurching out from Konia into the country, over the rough, rolling tracks, to carry to the people the food and clothes that would keep them alive.

The wonderful thing is that these camels were led by a Turk belonging to the people who hate the Armenians, yet he was carrying food and clothes to them! Why did this Turk in Konia go on countless journeys, travelling over thousands of miles with tens of thousands of parcels containing wheat for bread and new shirts and skirts and other clothes for the Armenians whom he had always hated, and never lose a single parcel?

Why did he do it?

This is the reason. Before the war when he was ill in the hospital Miss Cushman had nursed him with the help of her Armenian girls, and had made him better; he was so thankful that he would just run to do anything that she wished him to do.

To Stay or not to Stay?

But at last Miss Cushman--worn out with all this work--fell ill with a terrible fever. For some time it was not certain that she would not die of it; for a whole month she lay sick in great weakness. President Wilson had at this time broken off relations between America and Turkey. The Turk now thought of the American as an enemy; and Miss Cushman was an American. She was in peril. What was she to do?

"It is not safe to stay," said her friends. "You will be practically a prisoner of war. You will be at the mercy of the Turks. You know what the Turk is--as treacherous as he is cruel. They can, if they wish, rob you or deport you anywhere they like. Go now while the path is open--before it is too late. You are in the very middle of Turkey, hundreds of miles from any help. The dangers are terrible."

As soon as she was well enough Miss Cushman went to the Turkish Governor of Konia, a bitter Mohammedan who had organised the massacre of forty thousand Armenians, to say that she had been asked to go back to America.

"What shall you do if I stay?" she asked.

"I beg you to stay," said the Governor. "You shall be protected. You need have no fear."

"Your words are beautiful," she replied. "But if American and Turkey go to war you will deport me."

If she stayed she knew the risks under his rule. She was still weak from her illness. There was no colleague by her side to help her. There seemed to be every reason why she should sail away back to America. But as she sat thinking it over she saw before her the hospital full of wounded soldiers, the six hundred orphans who looked to her for help, the plain of a hundred villages to which she was sending food. No one could take her place.

Yet she was weak and tired after her illness and, in America, rest and home, friends and safety called to her.

"It was," she wrote later to her friends, "a heavy problem to know what to do with the orphans and other helpless people who depended on me for life."

What would you have done? What do you think she did? For what reason should she face these perils?

Not in the heat of battle, but in cool quiet thought, all alone among enemies, she saw her path and took it. She did not count her life her own. She was ready to give her life for her friends of all nations. She decided to stay in the heart of the enemies' country and serve her God and the children. Many a man has had the cross of Honour for an act that called for less calm courage. That deed showed her to be one of the great undecorated heroes and heroines of the lonely path.

So she stayed on.

From all over the Turkish Empire prisoners were sent to Konia. There was great confusion in dealing with them, so the people of Konia asked Miss Cushman to look after them; they even wrote to the Turkish Government at Constantinople to tell them to write to her to invite her to do this work. There was a regular hue and cry that she should be appointed, because everyone knew her strong will, her power of organising, her just treatment, her good judgment, and her loving heart. So at last she accepted the invitation. Prisoners of eleven different nationalities she helped--including British, French, Italian, Russian, Indians and Arabs. She arranged for the nursing of the sick, the feeding of the hungry, the freeing of some from prison.

She went on right through the war to the end and beyond the end, caring for her orphans, looking after the sick in hospital, sending food and clothes to all parts of the country, helping the prisoners. Without caring whether they were British or Turkish, Armenian or Indian, she gave her help to those who needed it. And because of her splendid courage thousands of boys and girls and men and women are alive and well, who--without her--would have starved and frozen to death.

To-day, in and around Konia (an Army officer who has been there tells us), the people do not say, "If Allah wills," but "If Miss Cushman wills!" It is that officer's way of letting us see how, through her brave daring, her love, and her hard work, that served everybody, British, Armenian, Turk, Indian, and Arab, she has become the uncrowned Queen of Konia, whose bidding all the people do because she only cares to serve them, not counting her own life dear to her.

FOOTNOTES:

[Footnote 64: In reading this part of the story to younger children discretion should be exercised. Some of the details on this page are horrible; but it is right that older children should realize the evil and how Miss Cushman's courage faced it.]

CHAPTER XXVII

ON THE DESERT CAMEL TRAIL

Archibald Forder (Time of Incident 1900-1901)

The Boy Who Listened An eight-year-old schoolboy sat one evening in a crowded meeting in Salisbury, his eyes wide open with wonder as he heard a bronzed and bearded man on the platform telling of his adventures in Africa. The man was Robert Moffat.

It was a hot summer night in August (1874). The walls of the building where the meeting was held seemed to have disappeared and the boy Archibald Forder could in imagination see "the plain of a thousand villages," that Livingstone had seen when this same Robert Moffat had called him to Africa many years before. As the boy Archibald heard Moffat he too wished to go out into the foreign field. Many things happened as he grew up; but he never forgot that evening.

At the age of thirteen he left home and was apprenticed to the grocery and baking business. In 1888 he married. At this time he read in a magazine about missionary work in Kerak beyond the River Jordan--in Moab among the Arabs--where a young married man ready to rough it was needed. He sailed with his wife for Kerak on September 3, 1891, and left Jerusalem by camel on September 30, on the four days' journey across Jordan to Kerak. Three times they were robbed by brigands on this journey. Mr. Forder worked there till 1896. He then left and travelled through America to secure support for an attempt to penetrate Central Arabia with the first effort to carry the Gospel of Jesus Christ there.

The story that follows tells how Forder made his pioneer journey into the Arabian desert.

The Adventure into the Desert Two pack-horses were stamping their hoofs impatiently outside a house in Jerusalem in the early morning a week or two before Christmas.[65] Inside the house a man was saying good-bye to his wife and his three children. He was dressed as an Arab, with a long scarf wrapped about his head and on the top the black rope of twisted goats' hair that the Arab puts on when he becomes a man.

"Will you be long, Father?" asked his little four-year-old boy.

The father could not answer, for he was going out from Jerusalem for hundreds of miles into the sun and the thirst of the desert, to the land of the fiercest Arabs--Moslems whose religion tells them that they must kill the infidel Christians. It was difficult to tear himself from his wife and his children and go out to face death in the desert. But he had come out here to carry to the Arab the story of Jesus Christ, who Himself had died on a Cross outside this very city.

So he kissed his little boy "good-bye," wrenched himself away, climbed on top of the load on one of the pack horses and rode out through the gate into the unknown. He thought as his horses picked their way down the road from Jerusalem toward Jericho of how Jesus Christ had been put to death in this very land. Over his left shoulder he saw the slopes of the Mount of Olives; down below across the ravine on his right was the Garden of Gethsemane. In a short time he was passing through Bethany where Mary and Martha lived. Down the steep winding road amongst the rocks he went, and took a cup of cold water at the inn of the Good Samaritan.

Then with the Wilderness of Desolation stretching its tawny tumbled desert hills away to the left, he moved onward, down and down until the road came out a thousand feet below sea-level among the huts and sheepfolds of Jericho, where he slept that night.

With his face toward the dawn that came up over the hills of Moab in the distance, he was off again over the plain with the Dead Sea on his right, across the swiftly flowing Jordan, and climbing the ravines that lead into the mountains of Gilead.

That night he stayed with a Circassian family in a little house of only one room into which were crowded his two horses, a mule, two donkeys, a yoke of oxen, some sheep and goats, a crowd of cocks and hens, four small dirty children and their father and mother; and a great multitude of fleas.

The mother fried him a supper of eggs with bread, and after it he showed them something that they had never seen before. He took out of his pack a copy of the New Testament translated into Arabic.[66] He read bits out of it and talked to them about the Love of God.

Early next morning, his saddle-bag stuffed with a batch of loaves which the woman had baked first thing in the morning specially for him, he set out again.

How could a whole batch of loaves be stuffed in one saddle-bag? The loaves are flat and circular like a pancake. The dough is spread on a kind of cushion, the woman takes up the cushion with the dough on it, pushes it through the opening and slaps the dough on the inner wall of a big mud oven (out of doors) that has been heated with a fire of twigs, and in a minute or two pushes the cushion in again and the cooked bread falls on to it.

So Forder climbed up the mountain track till he came out on the high plain. He saw the desert in front of him--like a vast rolling ocean of glowing gold it stretched away and away for close on a thousand miles eastward to the Persian Gulf. Forder knew that only here and there in all those blazing, sandy wastes were oases where men could build their houses round some well or little stream that soon lost itself in the sand. All the rest was desert across which man and beast must hurry or die of thirst. He must follow the camel-tracks from oasis to oasis, where they could find a well of water, therefore drink for man and camel, and date-palms.

So turning north he pressed on[67] till on the sixth day out from Jerusalem the clouds came up with the dawn, and hail and rain, carried by a biting east wind, beat down upon him. Lifting his eyes to the horizon he saw ahead the sturdy castle and thick walls of the ancient city of Bosra. Stumbling through the storm, along the narrow winding streets, he met, to his disgust, a man whose dress showed that he was a Turkish Government official. He knew that the Turkish Government would be against a Christian and a foreigner going into their land.

"Who are you?" asked the official, stopping him. "Where are you from? Where are you going?"

Forder told him, and the man said. "Come with me. I will find you and your horses shelter at the Governor's house." Forder followed him into a large room in the middle of which on the floor a fire was burning.

"I must examine all your cases," said the official. "Get up. Open your boxes."

"Never," said Forder. "This is not a custom-house."

"Your boxes are full of powder for arming the Arabs against the Turkish Government," replied the official.

"I will not open them," said Forder, "unless you bring me written orders from the Turkish Governor in Damascus and from the British Consul."

Off went the official to consult the headman (the equivalent of the Mayor) of the city. The headman came and asked many questions. At last he said:

"Well, my orders are to turn back all Europeans and not to let any stay in these parts. However, as you seem to be almost an Arab, may God go with you and give you peace."

So Forder and the headman of the ancient city of Bosra got talking together. Forder opened his satchel and drew out an Arabic New Testament, and together they read parts of the story of the life of Jesus Christ and talked about Him till ten o'clock at night. As the headman rose to go to his own rooms Forder offered to him, and he gladly took, the copy of the New Testament in Arabic to read for himself.

Saved by the Mist Next morning early, Forder had his horses loaded and started off with his face to the dawn. The track now led toward the great Castle of Sulkhund, which he saw looming up on the horizon twenty-five miles away, against the dull sky. But mist came down; wind, rain, and hail buffeted him; the horses, to escape the hail in their faces, turned aside, and the trail was lost. Mist hid everything. Forder's compass showed that he was going south; so he turned east again; but he could not strike the narrow, broken, stony trail.

Suddenly smoke could be seen, and then a hamlet of thirty houses loomed up. Forder opened a door and a voice came calling, "Welcome!" He went in and saw some Arabs crouching there out of the rain. A fire of dried manure was made; the smoke made Forder's eyes smart and the tears run down his cheeks. He changed into another man's clothes, and hung his own up in the smoke to dry.

"Where are we?" he asked. The men told him that he was about two and a half hours' ride from the castle and two hours off the track that he had left in the mist. The men came in from the other little houses to see the stranger and sip coffee. Forder again brought out an Arabic New Testament and found to his surprise that some of the men could read quite well and were very keen on his books. So they bought some of the Bibles from him. They had no money but paid him in dried figs, flour and eggs. At last they left him to curl up on the hard floor; and in spite of the cold and draughts and the many fleas he soon fell asleep.

As dawn came up he rose and started off: there (as he climbed out of the hollow in which the hamlet lay) he could see the Castle Sulkhund. He knew that the Turks did not want any foreigner to enter that land of the Arabs, and that if he were seen, he would certainly be ordered back. Yet he could not hide, for the path ran close under the castle, and on the wall strode the sentry. The plain was open; there was no way by which he could creep past.

At last he came to the hill on which the castle stood. At that very moment a dense mist came down; he walked along, lost the track, and found it again. Then there came a challenge from the sentry. He could not see the sentry or the sentry him. So he called back in Arabic that he was a friend, and so passed on in the mist. At last he was out on the open ground beyond both the castle and the little town by it. Five minutes later the mist blew away; the sun shone;

the castle was passed, and the open plains lay before him. The mist had saved him.

In an hour he came to a large town named Orman on the edge of the desert sandy plains; and here he stayed for some weeks. His horses were sent back to Jerusalem. Instead of towns and villages of huts, he would now find only the tents of wandering Arabs who had to keep moving to find bits of sparse growth for their few sheep and camels. While he was at Orman he managed to make friends with many of the Arabs and with their Chief. He asked the Chief to help him on toward Kaf--an oasis town across the desert.

"Don't go," the Chief and his people said, "the Arabs there are bad: when we go we never let our rifles out of our hands."

So the old Chief told him of the dangers of the desert; death from thirst or from the fiery Arabs of Kaf.

"I am trusting God to protect and keep me," said Forder. "I believe He will do so."

So Forder handed the Chief most of his money to take care of, and sewed up the rest into the waistband of his trousers. (It is as safe as a bank to hand your money to an Arab chief who has entertained you in his tent. If you have "eaten his salt" he will not betray or rob you. Absolute loyalty to your guest is the unwritten law that no true Arab ever breaks.)

The Caravan of Two Thousand Camels At last the old Chief very unwillingly called a man, told him to get a camel, load up Forder's things on it, and pass him on to the first Arab tent that he found. Two days passed before they found a group of Bedouin tents. He was allowed to sleep in a tent: but early in the morning he woke with a jump. The whole of the tent had fallen right on him; he crawled out. He saw the Arab women standing round; they had pulled the tent down.

"Why do you do this so early?" he asked.

"The men," they replied, "have ordered us to move to another place; they fear to give shelter to a Christian--one that is unclean and would cause trouble to come on us."

So the tribesmen with their women and flocks made off, leaving Forder, his guide, and the camel alone in the desert. That afternoon he found a tent and heard that a great caravan was expected to pass that night on the way to Kaf to get salt. Night fell; it was a full moon. Forder sat with the others in the tent doorway round the fire. A man ran up to them.

"I hear the bells of the camels," he said. Quickly Forder's goods were loaded on a camel. He jumped on top. He was led off into the open plain. Away across the desert clear in the moonlight came the dark mass of the caravan with the tinkle of innumerable bells.

Arabs galloped ahead of the caravan. They drew up their horses shouting, "Who are you? What do you want?" Then came fifty horsemen with long spears in their hands, rifles slung from their shoulders, swords hanging from their belts, and revolvers stuck in their robes. They were guarding the first section made up of four hundred camels. There were four sections, each guarded by fifty warriors.

As they passed, the man with Forder shouted out the names of friends of his who--he thought--would be in the caravan. Sixteen hundred camels passed in the moonlight, but still no answer came. Then the last section began to pass. The cry went up again of the names of the men. At last an answering shout was heard. The men they sought were found. Forder's guide explained who he was and that he wanted to go to Kaf. His baggage was swiftly shifted onto another camel, and in a few minutes he had mounted, and his camel was swinging along with two thousand others into the east.

For hour after hour the tireless camels swung on and on, tawny beasts on a tawny desert, under a silver moon that swam in a deep indigo sky in which a million stars sparkled. The moon slowly sank behind them; ahead the first flush of pink lighted the sky; but still they pushed on. At last at half-past six in the morning they stopped. Forder flung himself on the sand wrapped in his abba (his Arab cloak) and in a few seconds was asleep. In fifteen minutes, however, they awakened him. Already most of the camels had moved on. From dawn till noon, from noon under the blazing sun till half-past five in the afternoon, the camels moved on and on, "unhasting, unresting." As the camels were kneeling to be unloaded, a shout went up. Forder looking up saw ten robbers on horseback on a mound. Like the wind the caravan warriors galloped after them firing rapidly, and at last captured them and dragged them back to the camp.

"Start again," the command went round, and in fifteen minutes the two thousand camels swung grumbling and groaning out on the endless trail of the desert. The captured Arabs were marched in the centre. All through the night the caravan went on from moonrise to moonset, and through the morning from dawn till ten o'clock--for they dared not rest while the tribe from whom they had captured the prisoners could get near them. Then they released the captives and sent them back, for on the horizon they saw the green palms of Kaf, the city that they sought.

The camels had only rested for thirty minutes in forty hours.[68] With grunts of pleasure they dropped on their knees and were freed from their loads, and began hungrily to eat their food.

Forder leapt down and was so glad to be in Kaf that he ran into some palm gardens close by and sang "Praise God from Whom all blessings flow," jumped for joy, and then washed all the sweat and sand from himself in a hot spring of sulphur water.

Lying down on the floor of a little house to which he was shown, he slept, with his head on his saddlebags, all day till nearly sunset.

At sunset a gun was fired. The caravan was starting on its return journey. Forder's companions on the caravan came to him.

"Come back with us," they said. "Why will you stay with these cursed people of Kaf? They will surely kill you because you are a Christian."

It was hard to stay. But no Christian white man had ever been in that land before carrying the Good News of Jesus, and Forder had come out to risk his life for that very purpose. So he stayed.

What made Forder put his life in peril and stand the heat, vermin, and hate? Why try to make friends with these wild bandits? Why care about them at all?

He was a baker in his own country in England and might have gone on with this work. It was the love of Christ that gave him the love of all men, and, in obeying His command to "Go into all the world," he found adventure, made friends, and left with them the Good News in the New Testament.

FOOTNOTES:

[Footnote 65: Thursday morning, December 13, 1900.]

[Footnote 66: Recall Henry Martyn and Sabat at work on this.]

[Footnote 67: Passing Es-Salt (Ramoth Gilead), Gerash and Edrei in Bashan.]

[Footnote 68: It took the caravan six days to go back.]

CHAPTER XXVIII

THE FRIEND OF THE ARAB

Archibald Forder (Date of Incident, 1901)

The Lone Trail of Friendship So the two thousand camels swung out on the homeward trail. Forder now was alone in Kaf.

"Never," he says, "shall I forget the feeling of loneliness that came over me as I made my way back to my room. The thought that I was the only Christian in the whole district was one that I cannot well describe."

As Forder passed a group of Arabs he heard them muttering to one another, "_Nisraney_[69]--one of the cursed ones--the enemy of Allah!" He remembered that he had been warned that the Arabs of Kaf were fierce, bigoted Moslems who would slay a Christian at sight. But he put on a brave front and went to the Chief's house. There he sat down with the men on the ground and began to eat with them from a great iron pot a hot, slimy, greasy savoury, and then sipped coffee with them.

"Why have you come here?" they asked him.

"My desire is," he replied, "to pass on to the Jowf."

Now the Jowf is the largest town in the Syrian desert--the most important in all Northern Arabia. From there camel caravans go north, south, east, and west. Forder could see how his Arabic New Testaments would be carried from that city to all the camel tracks of Arabia.

"The Jowf is eleven days' camel ride away there," they said, pointing to the south-east.

[Illustration: FORDER'S JOURNEY TO THE JOWF.]

"Go back to Orman," said the Chief, whose name was Mohammed-el-Bady, "it is at your peril that you go forward."

He sent a servant to bring in the headman of his caravan. "This Nisraney wishes to go with the caravan to the Jowf," said the Chief. "What do you think of it?"

"If I took a Christian to the Jowf," replied the caravan leader, "I am afraid Johar the Chief there would kill me for doing such a thing. I cannot do it."

"Yes," another said, turning to Forder, "if you ever want to see the Jowf you must turn Moslem, as no Christian would be allowed to live there many days."

"Well," said the Chief, closing the discussion, "I will see more about this to-morrow."

As the men sat smoking round the fire Forder pulled a book out from his pouch. They watched him curiously.

"Can any of you read?" he asked. There were a number who could; so Forder opened the book--which was an Arabic New Testament--at St. John's Gospel, Chapter III.

"Will you read?" he asked.

So the Arab read in his own language this chapter. As we read the chapter through ourselves it is interesting to wonder which of the verses would be most easily understood by the Arabs. When the Arab who was reading came to the words:

"God so loved the world that He gave His only begotten Son, that whosoever believeth in Him should not perish, but have everlasting life," Forder talked to them telling what the words meant. They listened very closely and asked many questions. It was all quite new to them.

"Will you give me the book?" asked the Arab who was reading. Forder knew that he would only value it if he bought it, so he sold it to him for some dates, and eight or nine men bought copies from him.

Next day the Chief tried to get other passing Arabs to conduct Forder to the Jowf, but none would take the risk. So at last he lent him two of his own servants to lead him to Ithera--an oasis four hours' camel ride across the desert. So away they went across the desert and in the late afternoon saw the palms of Ithera.

"We have brought you a Christian," shouted the servants as they led Forder into a room full of men, and dumped his goods down on the floor. "We stick him on to you; do what you can with him."

"This is neither a Christian, nor a Jew, nor an infidel," shouted one of the men, "but a pig." He did not know that Forder understood Arabic.

"Men," he replied boldly, "I am neither pig, infidel, nor Jew. I am a Christian, one that worships God, the same God as you do."

"If you are a Christian," exclaimed the old Chief, "go and sit among the cattle!" So Forder went to the further end of the room and sat between an old white mare and a camel.

Soon a man came in, and walking over to Forder put his hand out and shook his. He sat down by him and, talking very quietly so that the others should not hear, said: "Who are you, and from where do you come?"

"From Jerusalem," said Forder. "I am a Christian preacher."

"If you value your life," went on the stranger, "you will get out of this as quickly as you can, or the men, who are a bad lot, will kill you. I am a Druze[70] but I pretend to be a Moslem."

"What sort of a man is the Chief of Ithera?" asked Forder.

"Very kind," was the reply. So the friendly stranger went out. Forder listened carefully to the talk.

"Let us cut his throat while he is asleep," said one man.

"No," said the Chief. "I will not have the blood of a Christian on my house and town."

"Let us poison his supper," said another. But the Chief would not agree.

"Drive him out into the desert to die of hunger and thirst," suggested a third. "No," said the Chief, whose name was Khy-Khevan, "we will leave him till the morning."

Forder was then called to share supper with the others, and afterwards the Chief led him out to the palm gardens, so that his evil influence should not make the beasts ill; half an hour later, fearing he would spoil the date-harvest by his presence, the Chief led him to a filthy tent where an old man lay with a disease so horrible that they had thrust him out of the village to die.

The next day Forder found that later in the week the old Chief himself was going to the Jowf. Ripping open the waistband of his trousers, Forder took out four French Napoleons (gold coins worth 16s. each) and went off to the Chief, whom he found alone in his guest room.

Walking up to him Forder held out the money saying, "If you will let me go to the Jowf with you, find me camel, water and food, I will give you these four pieces."

"Give them to me now," said Khy-Khevan, "and we will start after to-morrow."

"No," replied Forder, "you come outside, and before the men of the place I will give them to you; they must be witnesses." So in the presence of the men the bargain was made.

In the morning the camels were got together--about a hundred and twenty of them--with eighty men, some of whom came round Forder, and patting their daggers and guns said, "These things are for using on Christians. We shall leave your dead body in the sand if you do not change your religion and be a follower of Mohammed."

After these cheerful encouragements the caravan started at one o'clock. For four hours they travelled. Then a shout went up--"Look behind!"

Looking round Forder saw a wild troop of Bedouin robbers galloping after them as hard as they could ride. The camels were rushed together in a group: the men of Ithera fired on the robbers and went after them. After a short, sharp battle the robbers made off and the men settled down where they were for the night, during which they had to beat off another attack by the robbers.

Forder said, "What brave fellows you are!" This praise pleased them immensely, and they began to be friendly with him, and forgot that they had meant to leave his dead body in the desert, though they still told him he would be killed at the Jowf. For three days they travelled on without finding any water, and even on the fourth day they only found it by digging up the sand with their fingers till they had made a hole over six feet deep where they found some.

In the Heart of the Desert At last Forder saw the great mass of the old castle, "no one knows how old," that guards the Jowf[71] that great isolated city with its thousands of lovely green date palms in the heart of the tremendous ocean of desert.

Men, women and children came pouring out to meet their friends: for a desert city is like a port to which the wilderness is the ocean, and the caravan of camels is the ship, and the friends go down as men do to the harbour to meet friends from across the sea.

"May Allah curse him!" they cried, scowling, when they heard that a Christian stranger was in the caravan. "The enemy of Allah and the prophet! Unclean! Infidel!"

Johar, the great Chief of the Jowf, commanded that Forder should be brought into his presence, and proceeded to question him:

"Did you come over here alone?"

"Yes," he answered.

"Were you not afraid?"

"No," he replied.

"Have you no fear of anyone?"

"Yes, I fear God and the devil."

"Do you not fear me?"

"No."

"But I could cut your head off."

"Yes," answered Forder, "I know you could. But you wouldn't treat a guest thus."

"You must become a follower of Mohammed," said Johar, "for we are taught to kill Christians. Say to me, 'There is no God but God and Mohammed is His prophet' and I will give you wives and camels and a house and palms." Everybody sat listening for the answer. Forder paused and prayed in silence for a few seconds, for he knew that on his answer life or death would depend.

"Chief Johar," said Forder, "if you were in the land of the Christians, the guest of the monarch, and if the ruler asked you to become a Christian and give up your religion would you do it?"

"No," said Johar proudly, "not if the ruler had my head cut off."

"Secondly," he said to Johar, "which do you think it best to do, to please God or to please man?"

"To please God," said the Chief.

"Johar," said Forder, "I am just like you; I cannot change my religion, not if you cut off two heads; and I must please God by remaining a Christian.... I cannot do what you ask me. It is impossible." Johar rose up and went out much displeased.

"Kill the Christian!"

One day soon after this there was fierce anger because the mud tower in which Johar was sitting fell in, and Johar was covered with the debris. "This is the Christian's doing," someone cried. "He looked at the tower and bewitched it, so it has fallen." At once the cry was raised, "Kill the Christian-- kill him--kill him! The Christian! The Christian!"

An angry mob dashed toward Forder with clubs, daggers and revolvers. He stood still awaiting them. They were within eighty yards when, to his own amazement, three men came from behind him, and standing in front of Forder between him and his assailants pulled out their revolvers and shouted, "Not one of you come near this Christian!" The murderous crowd halted. Forder slowly walked backwards toward his room, his defenders doing the same, and the crowd melted away.

He then turned to his three defenders and said, "What made you come to defend me as you did?"

"We have been to India," they answered, "and we have seen the Christians there, and we know that they do no harm to any man. We have also seen the effect of the rule of you English in that land and in Egypt, and we will always help Christians when we can. We wish the English would come here; Christians are better than Moslems."

* * * * *

Other adventures came to Forder in the Jowf, and he read the New Testament with some of the men who bought the books from him to read. At last Khy-Khevan, the Chief of Ithera, who had brought Forder to the Jowf, said that he must go back, and Forder, who had now learned what he wished about the Jowf, and had put the books of the Gospel into the hands of the men, decided to return to his wife and boys in Jerusalem to prepare to bring them over to live with him in that land of the Arabs. So he said farewell to the Chief Johar, and rode away on a camel with Khy-Khevan. Many things he suffered--from fever and hunger, from heat and thirst, and vermin. But at last he reached Jerusalem once more; and his little four-year-old boy clapped hands with joy as he saw his father come back after those long months of peril and hardship.

Fifteen hundred miles he had ridden on horse and camel, or walked. Two hundred and fifty Arabic Gospels and Psalms had been sold to people who had never seen them before. Hundreds of men and women had heard him tell them of the love of Jesus. And friends had been made among Arabs all over those desert tracks, to whom he could go back again in the days that were to come. The Arabs of the Syrian Desert all think of Archibald Forder to-day as their friend and listen to him because he has proved to them that he wishes them well.

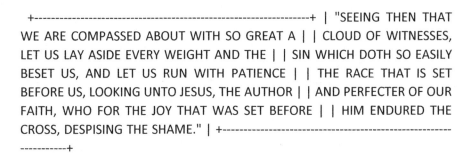

+--+ | "SEEING THEN THAT WE ARE COMPASSED ABOUT WITH SO GREAT A | | CLOUD OF WITNESSES, LET US LAY ASIDE EVERY WEIGHT AND THE | | SIN WHICH DOTH SO EASILY BESET US, AND LET US RUN WITH PATIENCE | | THE RACE THAT IS SET BEFORE US, LOOKING UNTO JESUS, THE AUTHOR | | AND PERFECTER OF OUR FAITH, WHO FOR THE JOY THAT WAS SET BEFORE | | HIM ENDURED THE CROSS, DESPISING THE SHAME." | +-- -----------+

FOOTNOTES:

[Footnote 69: That is Nasarene (or _Christian_).]

[Footnote 70: The Druzes are a separate nation and sect whose religion is a kind of Islam mixed with relics of old Eastern faiths, _e.g._, sun-worship.]

[Footnote 71: The Jowf is a large oasis town with about 40,000 inhabitants, about 250 miles from the edge of the desert. The water supply is drawn up by camels from deep down in the earth.]

###

Made in the USA
Coppell, TX
11 September 2024

37100882R00108